The Salt Doll

MOLLY DANIELS RAMANUJAN

women
UNLIMITED
an associate of
kali for women

The Salt Doll
was originally published in India in 1978
by Vikas Publishing House
This edition published in 2018
by
Women Unlimited
(an associate of Kali for Women)
7/10, First Floor, Sarvapriya Vihar
New Delhi 110016

www.womenunlimited.net

ISBN: 978-93-85606-17-5

Cover design: Sunandini Banerjee
Cover paintings: Mahmud Lashkar

Typeset by Manmohan Kumar, Delhi – 110035
and printed at Chaman Offset, New Delhi – 110 002

MOLLY DANIELS RAMANUJAN is the author of *Yellow Fish*, translated into Kannada by her husband, A.K. Ramanujan, and published as *Haladi Meenu*. She has also written *A City of Children and Other Stories*, two books of criticism, and a creative writing manual, in addition to editing eight books of poetry and prose. Her writings have appeared in *Chicago Review*, *The Carleton Miscellany*, *Experiments in Prose*, *Journal of Literary Studies* and *Primavera II*. An excerpt from *The Salt Doll* in *Tri-Quarterly* won her the Illinois Arts Council Award for fiction. She was also the recipient of the PEN Syndicated Fiction Award. An inspiring teacher, Daniels Ramanujan taught fiction and poetry writing in the Continuing Education Program at the University of Chicago and founded her own school, The Clothesline School of Writing in Chicago, mentoring 3,000 writers between 1979 and 1999. She passed away in 2015.

The Salt Doll *is brilliant. It comes at you in a rush of searing scenes that are utterly original. Daniels' fierce, poetic telling of a young woman's struggle to understand herself in a world ruled by gender and caste is unforgettable. I loved this book. When I finished the last page, I promptly turned to the beginning to savour it again.*

—Nancy Horan,
Author of *Loving Frank*

Situations in The Salt Doll *may indeed seem random, because Daniels is not interested in the ordinary trajectories of social experience or of personal development. Her "randomness" is an element of a cumulative narrative progress, one which proves a character's integrity by submitting her to an assortment of sufferings that emphasise her unremitting acceptance of herself, of what life inflicts, and of what it offers. That is the essential point of this ... glorious book.*

—Alane Rollings,
Chicago Review

To my husband,

Attipat Krishnaswamy Ramanujan

BOOK ONE

I

Mother left me when I was four. She did not just leave. She carefully thought up a strategy. She sent two maids and a coolie with me, to buy toys. She walked with us as far as the Kuttapuzha river.

The compound around the house on the rise dazzled white from the river sand, brought there periodically by hired coolies. The steps running down to the stream at the edge of the compound were interrupted by long stretches of whiteness, and lined with mulla and cock's tail and marigold.

Around the edges of the compound were the coconut palms and at the four corners, groves of cashew, jackfruit, and mango trees. We reached the little stream and crossed over the coconut trunk that served as a bridge across it. We walked single file across the clay ridges of several paddy fields and came to the river.

She stopped in the shade of a palm and leaning against its trunk pressed me to her round breasts. Her sharp nipples tickled my nose and I sneezed. Her gazelle eyes flooded.

Later, that picture of Mother would return to me. She was wearing a white mundu and chatta, the dress of the Syrian Christians. The fanlike frill of her mundu stiffer than a dry areca frond, the rest of her flowed soft.

Poor Mother, I thought, she cannot bear me out of sight even for an hour.

I returned laden with toys. The coolie carried some, the maids the rest. We entered from the rear, through the rubber estates. The servants stopped on the kitchen verandah. I went through the stairwell of the attic, through long corridors and another verandah of that single-storeyed L-shaped house, calling out all the names that only Mother answered to. I reached the last door, with its hand-carved frame facing the river.

I saw that the luggage was gone and with it the jasmine perfume she wore. I saw, through the open door, the white banks of the Kuttapuzha river and the paddy between, rippling ripples of green, waving goodbyes forever. The compound around me dazzled white from the sand brought from the banks across the paddy.

I was four, but I did not cry; though such a ball of fire as I have never felt since exploded in my throat.

Grandmother came up to me and stammered in Malayalam, "*ade, ade, ade*" meaning "that, that, that," and "*appazhe appazhe, appazhe*" meaning "then, then, then." "*Ade appazhe, ade appazhe,*"—"that then, that then was that," said my grandmother.

I said hoarsely, "Never mention that woman to me again." As I said it, I looked at Grandmother. Her velvet face was impassive, her lidded eyes a mystery. I was well acquainted with only one feature about her, her earlobes. In her Hindu youth she had worn so much gold in her ears that her earlobes were loops through which I could put my fingers when I sat beside her.

Later I found out that Mother had gone to join her husband, the man I never met till I was too old to have a father. I was free. I will tell you a secret, all you dispossessed people. If you have no parents, you have freedom. Freedom usually resides in a one-way street. But now freedom is the freedom to chew another's dirty toenails. It is not the half-done but the half-suggested that is the root of the alchemy. Recognition of nuances is interior. When I touch black (brown?) I am back where I was born. It is a kind of incest, isn't it?

Grandmother. She was a strange one. She always sat with one side of her face turned the other way, away from everyone. I never knew till I was eighteen that her nose was once pierced to sparkle with diamonds, a Hindu practice. And there she was on the verandah of a Syrian Christian household, mother to six sons and four daughters, all married to Syrian Christians, and yet wasn't she singularly alone? In all the years I lived with her, no one, not even her children's connections by marriage into the Syrian fold, ever called to see her. If anyone ever taught me to travel light, she did. Not by her speech, for she rarely spoke, but by the life she lived; "let live" was her code.

She let me drink black coffee. I never touched a drop of milk. To this day I share the Japanese horror of milk as a body exudation. He who has never known mammary glands may be pardoned for thinking that; so Japanese women give their napes pride of place. But if milk was taboo for me, very little else was. Once on a half lit verandah when I was five, a man pulled me on his lap. I felt his tumescence tickle my thigh. I did not know why he turned stiff under me. I never saw him again.

I played outdoors in every kind of weather, and my pale skin turned dark brown. I rowed with boys in leaky boats, got bitten by leeches and watched them grow like berries—red with blood. Grandmother never said a word. I muse over my kaleidoscope, looking backward at paradise.

No lines of timber floated by that house on the river, but maypoles of dragonflies, tied to a thread, spun a prism in their wings in the gold-flattened afternoon. Knee deep, bitten by leeches, berries grown with blood, the finger fish flurried past the water snakes that floated like weeds to where the dark women without blouses (have you seen such breasts?) bent to the harvest song under the eyes (such eyes?) of the overseers....

One day I ran away, but Grandfather brought me back. As he held me by the ear, his hand was silken. He had a white beard and tall stoop, skin that was crinkled and soft to the touch like turtle eggs, and gold-flecked, aged blue eyes that saw everything. Surely he was God.

There was the ritual of drinking tea with him at 10:30, mid-mornings. He would wait till I was found and brought in, and we would drink together, Silver Beard and I, elected out of all his grandchildren for that honour. He must have known all about me.

He was the next to go. The day he died, I wasn't anywhere to be found. The night before he died, he sent for me. I could not follow a single word that Silver Beard said to me; it sounded "thoff-thoff-thoff" to me. Next morning, I hid from embarrassment. Search parties missed me because I was perched high in a cashew tree. I saw them hunt for me, but I did not budge. He had been bathed and laid out, his pale brow bound in cloth of gold, when, late in the evening, watching long trails of visitors, I descended from my perch in the tree.

I walked into the front room. I saw his brow spun in gold, penciled below by blue veins, his arms stilled in a cross. I blacked out. When I came to, I was lying on someone's starched white lap.

Next morning, we went with him through the silence of bird watchers in the woods. At the family cemetery I shrieked the loudest.

My eldest uncle, lowering the teak coffin into the grave, trembled and lost his denture.

As we came back, Grandmother, who had to stay at home according to convention, sat on the floor in a corner. She looked smaller than ever. Her eyes were dry, and it was to her that I addressed my perverse remark: "Now that Grandfather is gone, who is going to drink tea with me?" She was silent as usual.

I was eighteen and she too had been laid to rest when I discovered her history. She was born into a Hindu home. Wealthy, they said—definitely wealthy. Her brother, when just out of school, had smuggled a missionary into their land. There they held secret prayer meetings, and Grandmother was converted. One night, fearing discovery, she picked up her year-old daughter and, with her brothers and the missionary, walked out on her husband. They rowed south. Telling me this, my eldest aunt, the daughter of a Syrian Christian judge, said bitterly, "If she started out on God's work, why did she not stay that way?"

It is my guess that the change from a young girl in a wealthy Hindu home to a missionary's dependent did not suit this woman of aristocratic tastes. One day Grandmother was kneeling in prayer after a bath, a custom carried over from her Hindu days (Hindus perform puja after a bath). Her hair was streaming behind her, her delicate features turned up in prayer. One look at her and Grandfather, passing by, decided to marry her.

He was a Syrian Christian. His family believed their tree went back to the beginnings of the Christian era. Within a week he and my grandmother were married, ostracised, and disinherited.

It took decades before he was accepted back into his own community. He gave enormous dowries even for his sons who, according to convention, should have brought home their weight in gold. To get my mother married, he had to go to my father's house seventeen times. The marriage settlement was handsome.

But the laws of nature have their strange repetitive patterns. Grandmother's daughter by her Hindu husband was married off to a Syrian Christian bishop's brother, who thereby gained a reputation for eccentricity—and lived up to it thereafter. After producing nine children (one every year), he picked up his eldest son and vanished.

Soon after Grandfather's death, he arrived dressed in robes the colour of saffron, wearing prayer beads and carrying a begging bowl or kamandalu, his son beside him. They looked like a calendar picture of mythic creatures.

He had not only been converted to Hinduism, he had become a sanyasi. Thereafter, he spent his time translating Sanskrit texts into Malayalam, and earned his livelihood by doing carpentry (a Nazarene affectation?). When I last saw him he was sitting on a tiger skin staring into space. I showed him a poem I had written. He neighed like a horse and returned it to me. I never found out whether he had taken a vow of silence that day or was anti-me or anti-poem.

I did not dare ask his wife, who was scrubbing chatties under a tree outside their thatched hut. She was lean and sharp in features, a Nair by birth, but uncomplaining and quiet as no Nair woman need be. Nairs are a matriarchy. The male marries into the female's family; the wife's brother is the overlord, and the male stud can be sent about his business to his sister's house, if he has a sister.

My poem? You want to know what I wrote at eighteen? No harm. I promised you I would be faithful unto death, but when strangers look at me with your grey eyes, when strangers walk along the cobbled square, I become as one possessed. Other men have used the words you said were yours. They do not stammer as you did once, when underneath the moon you held your breath for want of words.

I had another uncle. He got drunk every night. One night as I was studying in the verandah, sitting at a round table in the round arc of light from a kerosene lamp, he came to me. He scraped gravel from his hair onto the table, and the grains were visible.

His eyes too were visible; they were like the eyes of my dead dog. His tongue too. And he fell into a dead faint across me.

He had gone to the family cemetery, carried a cross he had pulled out for a mile, and then put it down in the middle of the bridge across the little stream I played in. Gravel in the hair....

I think I had three mad aunts, all aunts by marriage. I saw one of them chained to a gazebo once. The chains came down from the ceiling. She made horrible guttural sounds and beckoned to me. I stood fascinated.

I saw that in madness her teeth gleamed longer; her hair was like hay. Near naked, lewd in gestures, she pawed the earth like a horse in fine mettle. I thought to myself, madness is when a person is herself, not what the world wants her to be. Since then I have been very tolerant of mad people.

I remember an incident. I was asleep. It was during the vacations. The sun streamed through the open window. A rough hand on my shoulder woke me up. As I looked up a voice said, "*Maranam*," which is Malayalam for death.

"You look just like your mother, and you sleep like her, face down. When mother and daughter look so alike, one of them must die!"

By the time my sleepy eyes focused on her, they had taken her away. She kept saying "*Maranam, maranam*." The word had a sonorous echo about it.

Glimpses of myself in family diaries. My drunken uncle thought it fit to record: "I saw Mira playing today. On the flagstones. Odd and even. Odd and even. There is a God. There is no God. When it came out 'There is a God,' she missed her prayers, she said. On other days, she prayed. I asked her whether her prayers were answered, and she said, 'Yes, always!'"

Another entry interests me: "Mira faints when she cries or laughs too much. Today I made her laugh. She fell in a dead faint. I poured a bucket of water on her. I am glad I didn't make her cry or they would have cackled at me."

The last time I remember fainting was when I went to see my parents. I was taken to Aden to join them. My father looked like Hitler. He had the same moustache, the same jerky military ways. In my mind I called him the High Command, and in my diary I had him under the code H.C. They lived in Crater. I ran away to Steamer Point and tried to get onto a boat taking passengers to the P & O lying at anchor. The police on the quay took me home. When we arrived, my father raised his hand to hit me, and I fell in a dead faint. After several such attempts, they sent me back to India to a boarding school—for Grandfather was dead and to Grandmother I was just one of dozens of grandchildren. I did not last long in any of the boarding schools. I went to eleven, a new one each year.

At the first boarding school, the nuns wanted us to be truthful. If we told lies, they powdered quinine and rubbed it on our tongues. The nuns were Portuguese.

At the second boarding school, the nuns told us not to pluck mangoes. But the Indian priests told the Indian Catholics that it was no sin to pluck mangoes and they need not confess. There was a gap between what the Indian priests did not consider sinful and what the good nuns thought heinous. Caught between two subversive currents, we plucked mangoes. So the nuns decided to mortify us. They passed a string through the mangoes and tied it around our necks and sent us to class. They thought the day scholars, who did not board with us, would laugh at us. Instead, we were a sensation. At recess, we sold a bite each to anyone who came along. Result? We got ill.

At the third boarding school, they did not want us to read anything that was on the Index. This stricture did not bother anyone else at the school, but it did me. It turned reading into a crusade, a declaration of independence. Not that I did not read for pleasure; till I was fifteen, what I loved most was fairy tales. But the censorship imposed by the Mother Superior impelled me to explore such forbidden material as Dumas, father and son. I wrote a theme on *The Three Musketeers* and handed it in instead of my French verbs. The Mother Superior sent for my mother, whose favourite book was of course the blessed Bible, also on the Index! But my mother was overcome by the Mother Superior's outrage at my philandering among forbidden books. She became sterner than the Mother Superior as I stood facing them in a closed room in the school.

As I looked out of the window, I saw the cemetery with all the crosses, statuary, and memorials cheek by jowl next to the Mother Superior's room. One inscription began, "Greater love hath no man ...." I was not penitent, merely appalled by my mother's expression. I toyed with an idea—should I expose Mother? Did she not read the Bible morning and evening? Did she not quote from it, sometimes movingly, as when she'd say something like "My children like olive trees around my table?" But then followed this ritual.

MOTHER SUPERIOR: Kneel down. (*I kneel down facing the low window and the memorials to the dead.*)

MOTHER SUPERIOR: Repeat after me: I promise, ...

M: I promise...

MOTHER SUPERIOR: Never to read a book...

M: Never to read a book... (*Surprise, indignation, voice begins to crack.*)

MOTHER SUPERIOR: Not approved by Mother Superior.

M: (*Sobs, sniffles, omits first word.*) ...approved by Mother Superior. (*Tears flow.*)

MOTHER: Crocodile tears!

M: (*Looking up.*) "*Et tu.*"

MOTHER SUPERIOR: Mira has real feelings. No, she has real feelings. (*Kindly, very kindly.*) You may rise.

M rises, not dubbed an initiate into the society of the spiritual elite but stabbed to the heart by this mother. It takes Mira years to realise that her mother is female incarnate. She has no shape or form; she is everything or nothing. She is fluid; pour her into any mould and she takes it. Set her in any group and she becomes it. Except that she is all impulse and all imagination, a child forever, to be brought up by her six children, each born at five-year intervals—with each child, she the mother again the child, reshaped and reared by the growing child, but as now, in the presence of the Mother Superior, superior to the child that raises her, by virtue of the very Presence in Front of Whom She Becomes It. Ideals and principles lie outside her nature. Shapeless as water, necessary as water, these were the good moments, but what about when she becomes pure air, beyond touch?

Lest I forget, I was that day given an imposition of a thousand lines: "I must not read anything not approved of by Mother Superior." I learnt to write with four pencils tied together. No one can decipher my handwriting to this day—I did too many impositions.

One day, in a mood of defiant experimentation we stood, some of us, on the tennis court, in the sun, with sliced onions in our armpits. We ran up a temperature and were sent to the infirmary, stinking and in a fever, but happy to have exercised our freedom, by however tortuous a manner, to be at the place we wanted, with the choicest of our companions, away from the world we suddenly found impossible to accept.

At the fourth boarding school, the principal's name was something that sounded like Sistermaryabilliya. We called her Billy for short. Everyone except Billy knew this. That year there was a new teacher for us. She wanted me to ask Billy's permission for something, since I was one of Billy's favourites.

"I will fix it with Billy," I said.

"What's that you said?" she asked sternly.

"I will fix it with Sistermaryabilliya."

"You did not! You called her Billy Cat!"

I was silent.

She thought for a while and said: "Go and tell the Reverend Sister Maryabilliya that you called her Billy Cat. Right this minute."

The class gasped. Billy had a fierce temper. She usually used the back of a brush to correct the wayward. And since she was very short of stature, she usually jumped into the air, and the brush landed on our outstretched palms, and if we withdrew our hands and she lost her balance, the number of brushes were multiplied. We had learnt to leave our hands stretched out like cadets presenting arms to a state guest.

As I was leaving the room, Miss Diaz called me back. She, even she, shuddered and said, "All right, you may go and report to Sister Germana."

I got to the chapel and rang for Sister Germana, one-two-three-pause-one, the bell for Sister Germana. Who do you think popped out of the door? The fearful Billy. She asked what I wanted. I stammered. Billy was kind. She had always been especially kind.

"Whath du you wanth?" she repeated a second time.

"I want to see Sister Germana."

"Whath du you wanth?" a third time. I cast about. I did not want to push my luck any further, and try as I might I could not think up a story, and there was that fleshless Miss Diaz with her determined jaw at the back of my mind.

"Sister," I said clearly, "by mistake, I called you Billy."

The blood rushed to her square Portuguese face. Her collar seemed to choke her. Her eyes popped out.

"I donth untherstanth whath you are saying. I donth wanth you to come here for no gooth reason. I will make you thake your thrunk on your headth and go thown the hill!" With that she slammed the door on my face.

I was an instant heroine with the entire community. All sorts of nuns—Indian, European—that evening strolled around the playground holding my hand, making me tell over and over what I said, what Billy said.

I was with Canossian nuns once. They were wonderful, but once in anger I wished beautiful Sister Casanti dead. The following week they led me into a chapel, and there was beautiful Sister Casanti laid out with tuberoses in her hands, laid out in state for all to mourn, on a raised coffin, in the middle of the chapel.

I shrieked and fell in a dead faint.

No one knew why.

From the convents, I travelled back and forth from Mount Abu and Simla and Ajmer, from Bombay and Bangalore to Kuttapuzha, where ferns left their imprint of talcum on your skin, and where crow flowers and touch-me-nots hung in my earlobes, and there was always green under my feet—and boys. All my cousins were male. I had five girl cousins, but their parents never sent them to Grandmother's for vacation. Home for vacation, I no longer lived on treetops, but sat in the dark attic.

The attic was very dark. I would go up there with a hurricane lamp. At one end of it, bananas were stored for ripening. In my early teens, I would sneak up and read my uncles' marginalia, in books hidden in an old red trunk. Each book may have belonged to several of my uncles, but so great was the stamp of their masculinity that they all read as one.

One uncle, Verghese, particularly fascinated me. I had heard some gossip about him. In those days there were serfs who lived on our land. They were *pelayars*. They never entered our compound. They saw to it that their shadows did not cross ours. They worked on the land, and we paid them in kind and gave them new clothes every new season. They lived at the edges of our property at various points of the compass.

One of the *pelayars* who lived at the northern end was called Velutha, meaning "white". White had a buxom woman. She, like her tribe, never wore any blouses, and I still remember her erect, bobbing breasts.

The story is that Uncle Verghese used to visit this woman. Actually, she had a daughter who looked like me, and her right eyelid drooped a little, like mine.

One day my parents sent me a fresh set of clothes, made in England. (My parents had no sense of patriotism; this was the very time Gandhiji was teaching Indians to boycott British-made textiles of exported raw cotton from India, shipped out for nothing and shipped in at exorbitant prices. While the nationalists wore handmade, handspun khadi, they sent little English dresses for Indian me.) I gave my old clothes, old parasol, old doll, and slippers to Eerkidathi. *Eer* literally means "nit" and *kidathi* meant "the daughter of a *pelayar* living on your land".

She went about one day dressed in my cast-off clothes.

And they said to her, "Where are you going, Mira Thampuratti?" They had mistaken her for me.

It sent chills down my spine, and to this day I cannot decide whether she is me, or I her, and if not why not, and whatever became of her....

Instead of thinking of my uncle as a villain, as everybody else did (especially my aunts by marriage who looked at Grandmother and whispered darkly, "A bad seed!"), I placed him high among my heroes.

I read the marginalia to discover him. Reading the books he had read, I used to get very excited and often had to run to the bathroom. I did not know Uncle Verghese very well, as he had been sent away from home to live with Grandmother's brother somewhere in the interior. He came home only when his marriage was arranged.

But the house that Grandfather built on top of the hill after he became a pauper (bankrupt after paying all those dowries—even for his six sons, who, after the custom of the community, should each have brought home his weight in gold as dowry) had no toilets attached. I had to run all the way to the outhouse.

I had to avoid detection in the attic, as I wasn't sure they would not sell the books by the pound to the rags-and-bones man. They would not understand my excitement, and they certainly would not want me to sit among the cobwebs all day, reading. So morbid, they would have said. There was an idea among the younger generation that any kind of reading or intellectual work was bad for one's health. Most of my cousins complained of headaches the moment they sat down to their homework. Their mothers were generally very sympathetic, quite sure that they did not want their children to go to college.

In this, my aunts were very unconventional. Poor farmers sold their land and mortgaged their property, raised pepper vines, and grew rubber trees and other cash crops to educate their children. (Part of the reason Kerala went communist is that there has been free public education in that state since 1801—even before the British had public education in England.)

In a state so passionately set on education—any education—my aunts were being unorthodox. Or plain crazy. I admired them. They had a vigor and zest to their ways, the liberal illiterates.

My cousin Mathai usually came up to the attic when he was on vacation. He was not interested in the marginalia, he was interested in me. When I told him of my secret treasure, he was not impressed. What he enjoyed was kind of stroking me.

He drew rings around my breasts; he breathed on my neck.

We rubbed our noses together, though even then I had my eyes glued to the books. It made the whole thing a great adventure.

I was afraid I would speak in my sleep or blurt the whole thing out while talking of something else. I could never keep secrets—even now I cannot; that is why I write or talk. I feel a kind of bottomless pit inside me, never knowing what will come up next.

We were very innocent about the stroking and fondling. We did not know the facts, but blundered in a delicious sort of way and found out about touching and not touching, looking into the eyes and not looking. We also learnt to speak low and in a slow manner, glancing up and saying something slowly and softly, the division between speech and silence, speech and act, all blurred there in the half light, with bananas in proliferation at one end, the red trunk, the hurricane lamp, the rafters, the cobwebs, the dust, the fact that we did not know the facts. Later, away from the attic, memory would swirl up and down the cells of my awakening body, pulsing warm, shooting sharp delight into that region I knew as the heart. I knew all the exciting and excitable areas of my body. My thighs were electric, the nape of the neck a precious spot (the Japanese are right), and my breasts made me feel I would go up in smoke and be found out burning in the attic for all to see.

We did not know anything about kissing, not having seen anyone kiss. There were no English movies for us in those days. Neither did we know about being naked. It had not occurred to us. In a way I am glad. Incest is the greatest taboo among Syrian Christians; we cannot cross the incest line for five generations, and aren't we all literalists? Who would care if I thrilled to my cousin's touch? But who among anyone I knew would pardon me if I lay naked with him? Think of what the nuns would say! Even later, when understanding dawned on me, I never felt any guilt about the trips to the attic. That was prehistory, the Golden Age. It was a way of finding out something about myself. I do not think I can fully describe the effects of those episodes. I think they instilled in me a sense of privacy; everything till then had been public. They were soothing and dark, quiet and whispering. They changed me from a noisy brat to what I thought was a mystery woman.

Years later, I realised that all this had a deeper impact. In my flight from Eden, I travelled on a freedom road that was a one-way street; it took me years to realise that freedom is freedom to even bite another's dirty toenails. Recognition of nuances is interior. It is not the half-done but the half-suggested that is the source of the alchemy. When I touch truly, I am back where I was born. Only the dispossessed know what it is to return briefly. For embracing arms cannot reach the day the axe lay still against the yellow stump of a jackfruit tree or the day the dog was caught in a sealed oven of latex, bulging eyes fixed on a tongue held out for breath. *Kuriyelaiso*—Grandfather's brow bound in silk, his brow penciled by blue veins, the arabesque of arms stilled in a cross—went through the silence of birdwatchers in the woods. *Kuriyelaiso.*

2

THE *S.S. RAWALPINDI* SAILED FROM COCHIN TO ADEN.

The Raja of Cochin is a Nair, his wife a Brahmin; only a Brahmin can cook for a king, but the Rani does not cook; they have cooks.

The logic is simple: if they were stranded on a desert island, she could cook.

But Hindus did not travel by sea for many centuries.

Tamils (Dravidians!) went as far as Java; they left behind them words of Tamil origin, legends, and skills.

The rule is simple; anything complex can be reduced to a simple axiom: "Any remark made about India, any part of India, of any Indian living abroad, requires the opposite or the contrary to be stated about the same subject, the same region."

People flee from black, from night, from death, from dirt.

On the *S.S. Rawalpindi*, I discover the rewards of being black.

I am eight years old; I am put on the boat with a single box; I get off the boat with a dozen boxes. Pale Australians, who will not let Indians into their land, shower me with gifts, for I am black.

It is said of travellers going east that they hung up their souls at the Suez and picked them up on the way home. It could be said that the Australians get theirs only on the open sea. What is it that fills the heart with romance on a long journey by boat or train?

Or is it that regardless of the colour of my skin, they find me as delightful as a performing monkey and about as human?

My travelling companion, Miss Skinner, lets me eat at every meal, tapioca pudding with my fingers.

"I eat nothing but tapioca pudding," I tell her.

To keep healthy, a Punjabi I know eats five raw almonds first thing in the morning.

A Sindhi I know swallows a whole garlic. Mahatma Gandhi eats a whole plateful; he is worth a whole bunch of Sindhis.

The Parsis eat a few dates every day; that keeps them healthy.

Madrasis eat asafoetida once a day; a Greek friend thinks this is an aphrodisiac.

Old Tamil kings kept Greek and Roman women as mistresses. If the Nizam were to sleep with a wife a day, assuming that he could not sleep with a woman more than once a day (I am not casting any aspersions on him, but rulers I assume are busy people), it could take him a whole year to get back to her; what did she do meantime?

To say that Indian women are virtuous is to say nothing; why does a widow have to give up lentils, onion, garlic? Are lentils aphrodisiac?

Onion, according to ancient Egyptians, cured all common colds, and garlic, says medicine ancient and modern, is anathema to mosquitoes breeding.

To send a grieving widow posthaste after her absent spouse is no thought. Rebirth does not involve marriage to the same spouse. Think of the twenty-eight lakhs of spouses each one is entitled to, that is in the normal course of events. If you are particularly gifted, you can leap from a worm-in-dung to a man, and from man to God, in a few moves, but think of the fun you'd be missing.

Miss Skinner refuses to wipe my bottom; I am used to such services from servants in Kuttapuzha; she agrees to bathe me.

The sand-polished rocks of Aden look to me a herd of elephants. As I walk down the gangway everyone knows they are elephants. To me they look like rocks.

Not a blade, not a leaf, nothing grows here; I have come alone from Eden to Aden, goodbye!

As I walk down the gangway, I am back at Kuttapuzha; on my way to school, I stop and pick up two stones.

One is Chacko. The other Mira.

I lay them side by side.

"Now you be friends!"

I come back hours later; they are there, close and warm.

At the quay, H.C. and Rahel are waiting for me. I get a shock. They are not beautiful. I don't look at their faces; their car looks prettier than them.

"'Where's Chacko?"

"He is at home with Hamid."

"And what is Hamid?"

"He is a bearer."

"What is a bearer? What does he bear?"

The Madrasis don't eat asafoetida just like that. It is put into sambar. Sambar is a dish that when served at table looks to an English nurse like something familiar unfamiliar, eureka! She gets it!

"I know what it looks like! An abortion!" The nurse has abortion on her mind. She says, "I aborted a novel I wrote last year."

Rahel Cheriyan, who can be very literal-minded when she chooses, leaves the table and throws up. Years later, Rahel's second son, Idiculla, called this the yellow-teeth-syndrome. Idiculla too is a psychiatrist; rather effeminate of him, considering he is not a woman. To be a good novelist is to satisfy women. That is a man's job. But to be a psychiatrist is to be a mother, passive, loving, and breast-feeding. Most psychiatrists are men. Life is full of contraries.

Hamid is really an Arab Sheik from a small tribe in Yemen. He loves telling stories about Shaitan. He thinks a radish a day keeps the devil away; he nibbles radishes when he sits on a charpoy after lunch. On full moon nights he draws blood from Habib the cook. They fight and embrace with equal passion. Habib thinks Hamid is possessed of a devil.

H.C.'s family believe in devils; did they not kill their kinsman, the lame congressman who was their own flesh and blood, trying to exorcise him?

"Leave, leave the body of this good servant!" they said, meaning the servant of the Lord.

The lame congressman lost the elections and came home in a fever. If the devil had not got into him, would he have gone into politics?

The Nestorians are minorities, and if the majority cause is kept out of sight, there would be no loss.

Result? He died. They buried him, foaming with hosannas and halleluiahs.

H.C. keeps a cane. I ask R.C., "What is that cane for?"

"Hamid has the temper of a rogue elephant. We keep it to make sure he does not get out of hand."

"Do you use it on him?"

"No, oh no!"

Fair chance you will have. You will be reduced to ribbons. Have you seen the blade of that knife? Hamid has the aim of an archer with his knife; he sits all day on Sundays outside (it is not his Sabbath; his is on Friday), practicing his aim at stray cats. He never misses.

Fridays are for Muslims, Saturdays for Jews, Sundays for Christians. I wonder about Hindus, and I remember that Hindus have fifty-six festivals in a year. No one in Aden knows on which days these fall; only the pundits know; they consult panchangams printed in India, based on astrological calculations.

But the cane has a value all intrinsic. All the furniture in the living room is made of cane. If you live on a desert island, which is really a naval and military station for the British, you tend to use cane.

One hundred and fifty years earlier, an English poet wrote:

> Now came the cane, from India, smooth and bright with nature's varnish; sever'd into stripes that interlac'd each other, these supplied of texture from lattice-work that brac'd the new machine, and it became a chair, but restless was the chair; the back erect distressed the weary loins, that felt no ease; that press'd it, and the feet hung dangling down, anxious in vain to find the distant floor.

I knew he was talking of the chair, but was he too as short as Alexander Pope and me, his posterior as tender as ours?

> These for the rich: (H.C. lived rich, always!) the rest, whom fate had plac'd in modest mediocrity, content with base materials, sat on well-tanned hides, obdurate and unyielding, glass smooth, with here and there a tuft of crimson yarn or scarlet crewel, in the cushion fixt: (R.C. collects cushions, H.C. canes) if cushion might be called what harder seemed....

Cowper did not share the Japanese horror for milk as a body exudation. I ask you, was Chesterfield right? Does a man who has been fed at birth with a wooden spoon really get roused at the sight of a wooden spoon?

Don't the Japanese give pride of place to napes? As a Japanese man approaches senility—they say—he shifts his glance from napes to breasts, the lean and slippered pantaloon. Sam Johnson's response to female bosoms in actresses' green rooms was bowdlerised by Boswell in whose veins ran the blood of Bruce, much thinned.

Cowper cries out: "I was born of woman, and drew milk as sweet as charity, from human breasts." Whose human breasts? Did not Sam Johnson get his scrofula from a wet-nurse?

I read with a beating heart Cowper's testament as child, as man, as poet, as everyman. He knows he thinks, he knows he articulates, laughs and weeps, and exercises all functions of a man. How then should he and any other man be strangers to one another, mothers, fathers, brothers, sisters, nuns, priests, Arab servants? You want proof?

Cowper says:

> Can I rest as silent witness of the headlong rage, or heedless folly by which thousands die, bone of my bone, and kindred souls to mine?

I copy on a card for my desk:

> SHE BRINGS HER INFANTS FORTH WITH MANY SMILES BUT, ONCE DELIVERED, KILLS THEM WITH A FROWN.

H.C.'s father truly believed that reading anything other than the Great Book poisoned the mind. He would not let his children go for higher learning. H.C. left for Aden, when he found out that they would not let him use the dowry he had earned by marrying R.C., towards a medical education.

"Become a doctor?" roared H.C.'s father. "The Lord is the healer!"

Chacko has large eyes, biscuit-coloured skin, and a watchful manner.

It is summer. A sandstorm rages outside. I am reading a book. The house is sealed up; still the dust swirls in every shaft of sunlight and settles in my nostrils, in my nails, in the whorls of my ears. I long for cool moss, ferns with talcum on the undersides. Many-hued lantanas, and touch-me-nots for buttonholes.

The cottage by the sea at the northern end of the island has four neighbours. Mr Cheese lives in the first one. He drops his h's. I know a sentence he could render thus:

> O'ilda, 'ow 'orrible to go to 'ospital in 'igh 'eels in such a 'urry over all that sand!

I will tell you a secret: I don't think he really drops his h's all the time; I think he drops them only when he talks to Rahel Cheriyan. Everyone finds R.C. very handsome. Even beautiful. My memory is of an afternoon in the Sheikh O'Man gardens. The sunlight seeps through and speckles everything. R.C. is sewing a burgundy velvet skirt for my birthday next day, and looking at her while she talks to the men around her, I find her distinctly ugly, and feel guilty for thinking so. But Mr Cheese is under her spell.

In the cottage facing east are Batliboys; they use chalk powder to make motifs on their doorstep, and their speech sounds:

> *Nathi oudu jai, nathi oudu jai.*

They don't like to die in Aden; would like to go to India and die, even though there is a Well of Death in Aden. Parsis get the vultures to pick their bones clean after they are dead, but the sea does the same; water too can pick the flesh off bones—I wonder about the Zoroashtrians on the *Pequod*. To each his own way of disposing his flesh.

The Hindus, who share the cottage with them, have no problem disposing the dead; they pour pure melted butter and use sandalwood to broil bodies to the bone. The mandala on the doorstep of the Hindus is made from powdered rice. Hindus practice largesse where they can least afford it. This particular family comes from the

Punjab; their English is sapoken sallowly sallowly, a vowel between each consonant.

I lie with my book on a bamboo mat on the floor, which reminds me of my first sentence in school: in Kuttapuzha, at age three, on my first day, I learnt the sentence of all sentences—"The cat sat on a mat."

My eldest aunt said her first sentence in English was, "All cows eat grass."

I think they were preparing her to learn to read music, A, C, E, G. She says the sentence proudly now in her fiftieth year, for her first sentence in English was also her last.

My eldest uncle, Thommen, told me, "The first sentence a Japanese child is taught is—'The cherry blossoms are blooming.'

But if I had quit after my first sentence, I would have thought that the English spoke in rhymes.

Mother is out with Mr Cheese. The last time she was out in a storm with Mr Cheese who is tall and stoops, but still towers over Mother, she said, "Yes" and "No" to every remark he addressed in her direction, though she understood nothing.

The afternoon is hot, warmer than warm, dry as dry summer leaves; I lie on the floor. I get up and carry the table fan to the floor, and lying next to it fall asleep.

Prince Chacko comes in. He is three years old. He turns on the fan. He turns it off.

I am as quiet as Rousseau's sleeping gypsy and about as ignorant about electricity. In Kuttapuzha we used lanterns.

Chacko decides to take it apart.

I wake to screams and first aid. H.C. arrives, his dry tongue hanging out like a dog's, hot, mad, and frenetic.

The fan he twists into the shape of a modern abstract sculpture and throws into the sea.

The cane, till now Hamid's phobia, descends on me. I break out in welts. I will say this for the cane—a flexible rod made my will inflexible, my spirit stubborn; if today I am an angry woman, it is not because I menstruate once a month, or that my womb is tired from bearing young, or that I do not have something hanging between my thighs, but because children or women if they are passive, attract the beast in every man. Hamid, who deserved caning, never got it once; he wasn't even dismissed. Power resides in men only in small areas. H.C.'s power over me was absolute. He used it absolutely.

He says to Mother, "Rahel, look at the way they have raised her, wild and bold like the rest of them."

In Kuttapuzha, the unhusked coconut I picked out of a mountain of coconuts was called Chacko, and it stayed green on my table for a whole year. But the cane divides us from now on.

I am in love. I am in love, sings the blood in my veins. I love Carrot. His real name is not Carrot; I call him that because of his hair. He is six feet four inches tall; he is a captain in His Majesty's forces stationed in Aden.

I am spared the knowledge that he dotes on Mother. To me he said, "Ah, you're the girl I want to marry."

He gets H.C. off my back without knowing it. Carrot tucks me to bed, reads me stories. King Arthur and Robin Hood were heroes, but reading about the Green Hero, I am offended by the words they use; I start crying.

"How can they call such a man that!" I sob.

"What my love?" Carrot is puzzled.

"How can they call him bold!"

Carrot's face clears. He draws himself up to his full height. He looks every inch a hero; he holds his fist up, his uniform creases to reveal his biceps; he shouts out, "BOLD MEANS GOOD!" Bold means good, bold means good, wild means good too; my blood sings with joy. After that anything H.C. says is so much water off a duck's back.

Coming as I do from Kerala my v's and w's are all v's. Carrot sets me a task to stand on the shore and shout, the vide vide vorld, the vide vide vorld, and the v's become a w only with a kiss.

Hamid takes us by cab to the Sheikh O'Man gardens ten miles away. Every inch of soil in the garden has been brought from the mainland; these are the only trees in Aden. Seeing green again I become wilder and bolder. We were given ten rupees; I spent the return fare on ice cones, sherbet, cotton candy, balloons; we still have enough left over to return by cab. But that would prove I am wilder and bolder.

"No, Habib, the Shaitan will get you if you take us by cab."

I refuse to go by cab. I must walk. It is hot; it gets hotter as we start out. After a mile, Chacko will not walk any more. The Sheik carries him for another mile or two. The radishes he eats hold up till then. They will not walk any more. It is impossible to find a taxi between Mala and Steamer Point. A man comes by, carrying coal in sacks on a camel. With gestures and pleas I beg him to take Chacko on. To my disgust Hamid too climbs on it. They go off. I walk all the way back to Crater.

My reception is warm; this time the cane draws blood. Carrot is very pleased with me; such is the stuff that heroes are made of.

Mother bakes cakes; it must have been someone's birthday. Carrot begs her to let him ice the cakes. In British fashion, he licks his fingers, and just once the spatula he is using. My mouth waters. After he leaves, Mother gives away the cakes to Hamid and Habib.

"Let me eat them," I say.

"They are contaminated," she says. "The British are a very dirty lot. If a man has a spot on his face, he removes it with spit! They don't bathe; Mr Cheese smells like blue cheese!"

Mr Cheese has a niece, Hilda. She is a nurse. She is blonde. She says to Mother at a dinner cooked by Habib and served by Hamid, Mother resplendent in a chikan sari, green thread-work on grey, "Mrs Cheriyan, it must be hard to do housework in a sari."

Hilda is the daughter of a missionary and finds it hard to think that Mother has no work to do except look pretty, while she herself has to work taking care of Arabs like Habib and Hamid.

"I can do anything in a sari, climb a tree."

"There are no trees to climb around here," says Hilda. Mr Cheese is I think hard of hearing, because he does not hear any of it; he is smoking his pipe.

"Well, I can climb a ladder."

"Can you swim in a sari?"

"Oh yes, very easily."

"Won't it come in the way?"

H.C. who is not deaf, butts in now: "The sari is pneumatic."

Hilda's stubborn jaw sticks out.

"Can you save someone's life? Say, if a European woman was drowning, would you be able to save her life?"

"If a European woman is drowning, we just let her drown!" he says and turns to talk to Mr Batliboy who is going to expand his pharmacy at Steamer Point.

My stay with H.C. is cut short when Italy joins the war. Aden is now part of the war zone. On June 16, 1940, the Suez Canal is blocked and the bulk of the British fleet is moved to Gibralter and Aden. In Abyssinia, an Italian army of two hundred thousand men, cut off from their homeland, are fighting against a small British force. In North Africa, another two hundred thousand Italians are on the advance. The Germans are jubilant over the diversion. Overnight, the women and children of Aden are bundled into steamers. I am sorry to lose Carrot, but overjoyed to shed H.C.

At sea, Chacko starts crying every time we sit down to a meal.

"I want my daddy in *kappal*!" he wails, his vocabulary part Malayalam. It is just like mother to have taught her little prince a tenth of his words in Malayalam, so that he cannot make himself clear to anyone else.

To me he said in Arabic, "*Antha makhnoon fi*," which, if I remember correctly, means "You are mad".

Every time any child or woman starts to sniffle, the whole ship of two thousand women and children would start wailing. If I ever felt like joining them, it was because I remember Carrot's face on the pier.

Mother is very callous about Carrot. She even told me, between crying and praying and looking at the moon, saying, "Ah, that's the moon my husband sees!" that when she was sixteen an Englishman, who saw her escorted to school by her brothers, sent a proposal for her hand in marriage. She was sixteen then, and in haste her family sent out messengers to the four corners of Syrian Kerala that their daughter Rahel was ready to be united in holy matrimony.

The first proposal was that of H.C.'s family. They were spellbound by Grandfather and his wealth. They basked in the effulgence of his personality till they found out about Grandmother. They then changed their tune, and hid their faces.

Grandfather was going to Trivandrum to pursue another proposal when he got the idea that since Rahel had seen the young man from Elakattu, she should be asked how she felt about it. Grandmother was reluctant to find out, so she sent Ponnamma, the cook, to do so. Ponnamma came back with a message from Rahel. They were the words of a monomaniac.

"If I am ever to marry, this is the only man I shall marry!"

She had seen him for a few moments, but with this sentence she decided my entire life for me.

Grandfather went seventeen times. On the day of the agreement to unite the two Houses with this union, money bags were deposited as ample recompense. But when Father came for the engagement party, he took off the gold earrings, bracelets, bangles, yards of gold chain, and all the diamonds off mother, laid them in a neat pile, and said, "My people don't wear jewellery."

My aunts, listening in the next room, were stunned. "What! Is Rahel going to run about like a cow without a halter?" they cried.

To them, a woman without jewellery was practically naked. When young Cheriyan got home, his family was horrified; they said, "Why did you do that? We could have sold the jewellery and kept the money."

Eighteen was my year of enlightenment. I did some digging into H.C.'s antecedents, and therefore into my own. I had some inkling they were religious maniacs. The one occasion I visited them when I was ten, they made me kneel down at a family prayer-meeting and confess I was a sinner. They made me cry by telling me I was a sinner. I confessed I was one, and cried because of their compelling me to confess. They thought I truly wept and repented; they declared I was born again, and kept me in cotton wool for a whole day and a half.

I ran away after that to Kuttapuzha. But as I made inquiries I found out that six generations before me, two brothers got into trouble; the younger one, Ouseph, had killed a man in anger, and the older one, Mammen, his brother's keeper, took him south and hid him in Elakattu, then a jungle (*kattu* meaning literally a jungle). There they thought they could live the whole thing down, or rather, live it up.

H.C. claims descent from Mammen, the older brother, the one who was his brother's keeper. But I have my doubts, till I find out that the man killed in anger had a curse put on his House. And all the male progeny since then have died sudden, tragic deaths.

The surnames do not matter among the Syrian Nestorian; it is the House name or the property that identifies a man. So a whole village might very often have the same House name.

For generations, Arapura House was full of young and grieving widows. So fond was H.C.'s father of recounting the magical ways in which son after son of his rival House, produced with great urgency and in a bid to beat fate, were mauled by bulls, drowned by floods, struck by lightening and bitten by snakes (the Ayurvedic too arrived late with the antidote).

One young man, a medical student, was bitten by a mad dog, and despite the anti-rabies shot he took, barked his way to wherever the powers sent him.

Sons of Cain, innocent yet marked, they believed in spite of all this that there was a power higher than them that determined everything. They, in the liminologies of the primitive Christian spirit of the first century, living in terror of pagan Hindu India, evolved and recreated every Judaic myth—what thinking men, even six thousand years earlier, had perhaps not taken that literally.

Cannons sound all day at practice of target shots; we wear ear plugs. The sky is full of flying chips. We make detours. A ship in our convoy is sunk. We have drills on how to abandon ship; we put on our life belts, and get into boats.

The voice over the speaker says, "In a real emergency, don't wait for the boats, put on your life belts, and jump into the sea."

I don't know if they really said that; Mother thinks they did not, but that is what I understood, and the next time the siren went, a British sailor saved me from going overboard.

R.C. married H.C. because an Englishman sent a proposal when she was sixteen, and she remained sixteen ever after. Arrested development. But you can see why I do not hold that against the British.

Chacko and I play on deck. The journey takes twice as long. The evening sky is full of the figures of cloud. We see in the evening a zoo of animals in the sky.

We saw Moses descending with the ten commandments, the burning bush; we even saw the crucifixion and there was no dust storm to cloud our view.

I still dream of mulla and cock's tail, the patter of monsoon, mangoes falling in a storm, and still pools of water. Irrigation ditches of clay weaving cool arterial connections through green paddy, now bristly now yellow now sprout green now golden now threshed, always singing at harvest and sowing and replanting, and the outdoor feast with banana leaves for plates, sandalwood paste for cold cream and pine scent for sprinkling, jasmine in the garden, moonshine on white sand, the taste of dewdrops, rainwater beads on waterproof leaves that roll and run like spilled mercury as I sway giant stems of giant leaves, and the happy toads on lotus pads in green garden ponds, and lilies of every sort.

I even long to use once again the leaves we used instead of toilet paper, especially grown around the outhouse. I used to have my own outhouse built with thatch, that *I* used and no one else. The way I figured it, no one objects to their own smell, only to that of other people.

On the way by boat, and in the hotel in Bombay, the refugee's connections by rail, bus, and car; never stopping longer than a few days, looking for a place, a way of living, yet uncertain, she who had no communication with me till now got into long monologues. She never fails to call me Malapuram Thulukachi. This is feminine for Malapuram Thulukan. A Muslim from a certain area of Malabar. Sly, cunning, undependable, usually a fishmonger, and usually fishy.

My connection with these villains is that I was conceived in their coastal city of Calicut. So, like a chameleon, at the foetal stage I had acquired characteristics. Years later, when my hatred for H.C. and R.C. grew, I used to wish that I had been fathered by a passing stranger. Then it occurred to me that perhaps H.C. wasn't half as bad as her, that a child of hers conceived in Malapuram Thulukan country should have all the characteristics of a Malapuram Thulukan.

"The day you were born, your father lost his job."

"Which father?"

"When you came to live with us, we were evacuated."

"I am responsible for the War! Mussolini is my fault! His interest in Abyssinia is my fault!"

The litany always began abruptly and ended just as abruptly.

If touch was taboo for nuns, it was for Mother too. The last time she hugged me was when I was four. But she sang nursery rhymes in Malayalam to Chacko. One of them comes back to me.

Kakai, kakai, koodevidai
Koottinakathoru kunjundo
Kunjinoo theetti kodukanjal
Kunju kidannoo karanjeedum

Kunjai, kunjai neetharumo
Ninnudai, kaiyilai nayyappam
Ayyo kakai patticho

Kakai is Malayalam for a crow. Every time I return to India from Aden, the first thing that strikes me are the crows.

When a crow dies, a whole colony of crows collect and caw and mourn the death of their fellow. Black birds, glossy black birds, offal birds, yet capable of mourning the death of another crow, capable of stealing food from my plate to feed its young. Black bird *Kakai, Ayoo Kakai*, father crow, mother crow willing to steal even from a friend for the offspring waiting for your return. That is a paradigm for wonder in a nursery where there was neither parent.

Grandfather is dead, and to Grandmother I am just one of forty-eight others.

Mother, like a migratory bird, keeps moving to find a place not too humid so Chacko can breathe and I go off to boarding schools, to one every year of my years at school.

3

NUNS: INDIAN, EUROPEAN; TALL, SHORT, DARK, FAIR. NECK below is starched white linen; only the eyes glow.

They are medieval—every shade of expression gets conveyed on their faces. When their hands are not in use, they hide them in their ample sleeves, each palm crossed over to the opposite sleeve.

To see them ascend or descend a flight of stairs is to be transported into another age and another country.

I am deaf to anyone who says that they were raised like me. They sprang immortal, stayed that way, and went back to their eternal home, to the Lord they were wedded to.

I have a fantasy that my own mother was not born the natural way. Grandfather going for a walk in the morning, dressed in flowing white, leans on his carved walking stick. Bending over he sees out of the red earth two cabbage leaves. On closer examination they turn out to be Mother's ears.

They dug her out, and she was seasonal like the earth ever after.

Reverend Mother Sylvia has loose dentures. Every time she laughs her upper dentures fly out. With her right hand, chalk and all, she swiftly thrusts them back.

It does not occur to me that all she needs is a couple of trips to the dentist. Everything is supplied by the Lord, and is common property in the convent. The pen she uses is "our pen" and even her ruffled and starched collar and bonnet are "our collar" and "our bonnet". To test this Marxist view of property I ask her, "May I borrow *our* pen?"

"No, you may not!" she snaps with locked jaw, the teeth of course in place.

Perhaps dentures too are not specifically fitted for her; my mind runs off in class.

She is very unfair every time her dentures fly—she fixes me with a stare. Through her bifocals I can see an unmistakable signal—"I dare you to laugh!"

The whole class can laugh. I feel cheated. To be fair, I must admit that she looks at me every time she makes a point or asks a question.

Ordinarily this brings my mind back, puts some spark into me, but since she chokes my laughter off I start a game.

Every time she looks at me, I droop my left eyelid (my right eyelid has a natural sinister droop). With the left one down, I manage to look sleepy, bored, moronic.

I do this once too often, and suddenly flinging down the duster, and with her denture clapped in place she takes hold of my shoulders, forgetting the taboo against touch. She begins to shake me; she shakes me till my teeth begin to rattle. She says: "Christmas pudding! Jelly fish!"

She repeats those two phrases till both of us turn blue.

She straightens up. "From now on you sit near the door, on the last desk!"

The next teacher is Reverend Mother Superior, from southern Italy. She takes French. She stops at the door and demands sternly: "Who put this dissipated child near the door?"

"Mother Sylvia asked me to sit here."

"Why?"

"She thinks I distract her."

Her face brightens, "Yes, that's the word! I meant distracted, not dissipated. You are too easily distracted; you must not sit near the door; you sit on the desk facing mine."

I change places. When Mother Sylvia is due, I rush over to the desk by the door; both nuns are satisfied, and each thinks I sit where they see me sitting. So much of life is an illusion.

Italians do not speak English any better than Indians. This pleases us. Since we cannot murder the English, we are quite happy to settle for murdering the English language. An Englishman in India is very different from an Englishman in Aden or Tahiti.

It was certainly larger than a chamaeleon, in colour like one, and erect. I was terrified. The Matron was standing under the neem tree, and was watching me as I mailed her letter for her in the mailbox outside the gate, when I heard a rough Tommy voice say something to me, and in the same instant I saw him sitting in the gutter, his back against the convent walls, his khaki pants unzippered, open down his lap, and standing at attention, pink at the tips, with a kind of impertinent one-eyed stare was this abnormal penis nowhere like Chacko's, jerking up and down. So stunned was I, so filled with terror that I ran straight into Matron.

"You are a big girl now, you must walk like a lady," she said.

I was not a big girl yet; I was in the small girl's dormitory. But at that time I did not yet know that a girl is sent to the big girl's dormitory only when she starts menstruating.

In fact, no one ever explained about menstruation to me, till I began trickling blood.

"What is that spot on your tunic?" the Matron asked me.

"It is a wood mark from climbing trees," I told her.

By evening I was in tears: I thought I had dysentery. When Matron tried to explain to me the mystery of the monthly curse, or in the vocabulary of the big girl's dorm, getting your chum, I burst out, "Will my brother Chacko be menstruating?"

"No."

"That is very unfair, very very unfair."

I burst into tears. Yet, it did not seem such a curse. I thought that once a day, plop, a few drops of blood and that was it. But I gave way to sobs and a stream of tears when I found out that one did not just trickle once a day or twice a day, but continuously and nonstop for three to four days. A rawness settled inside me. I thought I trickled from the urethra. It is only when I passed clots that I realised it could not be from the bladder; it was as if miles divided the two sensations. I decided to make a thorough examination.

I smuggled a hand mirror wrapped in a towel to the bathroom. Squatting on the floor, sitting on the toilet, lying in the bath, from every angle I examined myself.

I stood up, and counted all the orifices of my body, and counting the navel, I had nine. So the Chinese were no different from Indians. I had read a Chinese novel where the heroine perfumes her nine orifices, and now I knew what they meant.

Mother Beatrice, Canossian nun, age unknown, took to long silences. On days she does not utter a sound; she writes on the board, and the chalk squeaks in her place. Days she takes her vow of silence, I am on trial. Deprived of touch and now of sound, the more silent she becomes the more I talk. A message on the blackboard reads: "All those who are talking in class go downstairs." Half the class gets up and troops out.

We stand under an arbour outside, and some of us chat. The gong sounds and the monitor comes to say: "All those who are not talking downstairs may return to class." A great many leave. The bell rings again, and only Bhanu Vakil and I are left.

"Bhanu, you listen, I will talk!" Bhanu Vakil disappears.

I am left alone; I eat a few leaves off the arbour, I give a couple of tendrils of ivy a pull. I go round the building. I wonder whether I should jump the low gate and go sit in the cemetery and read all the nineteenth century inscriptions. But there against the wall of my classroom is this rusty steel ladder fixed against the water tank on the flat roof. The mali uses this ladder to go to the water tank. I have never noticed the ladder before, or the tank.

I climb the ladder; midway by hanging on to it, I can peep into Mother Beatrice's classroom. I hang by my right hand, my left ear prickling for sound, but the silence of the cemetery reigns inside. I get bolder, I show my face at the window, and a tall girl sitting in the front, Zoe Gonsalves, flings her fountain pen down, her hands up as if stuck at gun point, her eyes saucer-wide; she screams out my name.

Mother Beatrice has a sprightly manner even when silent; she rises, swishes her skirt in a flare, takes a half turn and like a sailboat picks her way billowing down the aisle to the door at the other end. She thinks I am at the door, and no doubt plans to pull me in and make me stand in the corner with the dunce's cap, with the long tongue hanging out of the witch's cap like an obscene thing. This cap is for the lower school and to be made to use it is like being punished as well as demoted.

Waist up at the window, when I see Mother Beatrice spinning around like a Spanish dancer, I let go my hold; scraping my knee, tearing my pocket, I fall on the turf below. I pick my shaken bones and sprinting across the tennis court, hide myself in the church.

I sit and stare at the stations of the cross. I stare at the sanctuary. I make faces at that incredible Infant. The thought of diaper pins and diapers comes into my mind. I have another brother now; his name is Idiculla. Mother and Chacko are back in Aden.

Search parties are out for me. Mother Beatrice breaks her silence. When found, I am not expelled because I am found in the church on my knees.

"Penitent," says Mother Superior.

To placate my conscience I tell that diaperless Infant, "Baby, I won't talk in class again." I keep my word.

For me it never rains but pours. The chums does not leave me. It continues for a whole month. I am sent to Aden by plane. They try a transfusion; they say I lack male hormones. I react to the blood. They have probably not matched it right. I am given H.C.'s blood next. I take this as proof—my paternity is settled.

When return I am treated gently. H.C., stern man of few words, takes to stroking my body. Mother sees him.

"I saw your father put his hand over your breast," she said.

"Did he?" I said.

"Does he do that often?"

"Why don't you ask him?"

"I did ask him."

"Oh? What did he say?"

"He says that he does not know how to show affection to you. He has never seen you as a child in diapers, growing. In any case, breasts are just like hands." But from then on a kind of pendulum sets in.

Breasts are like hands.

They are not like hands.

And caught between these two, Mother finds herself smiling one day, weeping the next. On days she smiled she told me, eggs are bad for you, they are so heaty. Meat is bad for you, it is heaty. Persuaded, I give up all protein food and settle for a fare that would make prisoners riot.

I am sent back to India; one day when a Japanese high commissioner's wife showed us at school the art of bonsai, I understood, in retrospect, that Mother was performing bonsai on me. She would have loved me if I could be found on the nursery floor, a year old, and still in diapers.

My parents returned to India. H.C. has spent fourteen years in a desert.

"His brain is heated up," says Mother.

From then on, they seemed to thrive on moving. At first the excuse was that flats were not available in Bombay. They abominated owning anything like house or property; so they sold for a quarter of its value H.C.'s share of the land that came to him from his father. He sold it to his brother, who gave him twenty thousand rupees. H.C. was going through a crisis; he spent the sum at the race tracks. R.C. was going through a phase when she thought horses were IT.

They lived in two houses in Santa Cruz. They briefly shared a room with a Parsi egg seller, a mosquito net dividing the room. They lived in Byculla where the Anglo-Indian, who shared the flat with them, walked about naked in the house. They lived in Dadar with Syrian Christians, but moved out because the yard was a garbage dump. Mother could not live anywhere where they did not cook in pure butter. She could not eat anything that came out of a can, or contained pork or shellfish. She could not put her foot down unless the floors were mopped twice a day, the bathroom cleaned three times, the drapes washed once a week, and the tablecloths changed daily. The furniture had to go every season, and every member of the house had to bathe and wash their hair daily.

My vacations were spent with them only when, after two years of wandering, they finally got a flat of their own. Strangely enough on my sixteenth birthday, an Australian leaving town, in a moment of defiance against the Goan landlord, gave the flat to my father, while the landlord Frank Rozario wanted it for his son Maurice, who was getting married. They got a court order to vacate the premises when I got home for vacation. The landlord's favourite daughter Patsy found me as congenial as H. Haterr. She made her father withdraw the eviction notice. Frank did not last long. At his funeral I saw something that cooled my view of Patsy. The little angel made a speech and rolled her eyes at us.

"Oh my papa," she cried, darting a glance at me. "Oh my papa, you are there six feet deep and I am all alone!" But her mother loved her just as much, and she had an animated relationship with Yvonne, Enid and Maurice; they were a happy family!

On the floor above us lived a family of fourteen women, mother and thirteen daughters. I do not know why she chose this folklore number. No child resembled the other. They varied from blonde to dark, all of them were tall, but this was their only common feature. Their mother was Portuguese. But what began to fill me with a kind of creeping doublethink was the fact that the eldest Walker girl is called Scarlet, has a friend called Ashley, and marries another called Rhett. Ashley married a younger sister, slim and pale, called Melanie. This so intrigued me that unlike my mother's prayers, it was not the Walkers who wished this fable on Margaret Mitchell, but Margaret Mitchell who christened or re-christened these four after the manner of her own well-considered fantasy.

My mother's prayers were always predetermined. She spent the nine months of her pregnancy praying for a daughter. She had two sons, Chacko and Idiculla, but she longed for a daughter other than me. It is not that my mother did not know that sex is determined at the moment of conception, but so great is her faith at such moments that time and events are reversible. It is not merely that the good Lord would know what his servant desired, but that the good Lord would have granted the wish, because he knew that his servant would spend the next nine months of her life on her knees praying for an event that had already been determined by the infinite wisdom of His everpresent, everconscious, never failing knowledge of the minutest act of His servant, past, present and future. To be under such scrutiny and care must in a way account for the resilience and bounce of Rahel's thoughtless, unconscious and impulsive life.

There was another family below us, with the last name of Menezes. Their father Antony taught music. Their mother Cynthia was a seamstress. I have never seen her leave her sewing machine except to walk stiff-legged like a stork to St Francis Xavier church, wearing a hat with flowers and things.

When the Menezes family were at dinner (I happened to have gone there to borrow a book on the history of church music), to my amazement I noticed that they used phonograph records for place mats. They served soup and dessert, and home made raisin wine. They spoke Portuguese at home, spoke of visits to Lisbon, and were trying to live some continental myth of the struggling musician supported by the heroic seamstress.

Both the Walkers and they seemed to approximate in their slightest shade, events recorded elsewhere.

Ava Walker looks like Ava Gardner. She even talks like Ava Gardner. I saw an incredible picture of Ava in a fur-trimmed coat, descending an incredibly wide and elegant stairway; I don't know where they found so opulent a setting, and which viceregal lodge in which Himalayan resort provided the temperature and elegance of that setting. I have heard it said that in Miami they turn rooms into freezers, so the women can sport their furs. Yet the Walkers could not be dismissed as marionettes. I have never seen such life and energy in bodies that seem to have been conceived originally as line drawings with single lines, no matter what the movement.

The seventh Walker girl, the middle sister, Samantha, begins to fill my imagination. I never see her date the same man twice; if he showed his face at all, it was in line behind several cars that constantly stopped at the kerb and drove off, as if a glance at the edifice that housed this goddess was all they craved for. The man she married was seen only on the day of her wedding. Her body is like sculpture that has no shadow, both fluid and rocklike. She made beauty queens look like mannequins. She wore neither bra nor girdle and she showed not a trace in her face or bearing that she could not tell night from day, or one man from another. She proved to me that H.C.'s family were dead wrong; there was no retribution waiting for Samantha Walker.

Samantha turns up at our flat wearing a bikini; she parks herself on top of H.C.'s desk. H.C. held no threat for her; she could have tweaked his hooked nose, or made him stand on his head. Mother always wiped the telephone receiver with an antiseptic after Samantha used the phone.

Towards the creek near the slaughterhouse at Bandra is a small meadow. At the edge of it, a man with an umbrella over his head, a woman with an uneven hem for her sari, and an abstracted child were trying to make a buffalo get up from the water.

Beyond, waiting pail in hand, a little girl darts out between the legs of cattle and collects the fresh dung as it falls like pancakes.

Girl in dotted skirt, girl with an identity, the dung-collector of her family, looks sprightly. Could I be her, and could she be me? Once in Kuttapuzha, on the way to school, I made the servant girl exchange clothes with me, behind a hedge. Her *pavada* trailed in the dust, while mine reached just below her knees. I left her crouching behind the hedge trying to cover her bare calves, while her skirt trailed burrs and twigs into the classroom. I stop as I see a calf hardly weaned trying to mount a cow. Suddenly something I had wiped out from memory comes back. My heart begins to pound. The memory or dream I am forcing back is momentarily displaced by what I saw at night the previous week.

I wake up, and in my sleep-filled glance, in the street below, I see out of my window the originals of all who went into the Ark.

The Arabs thought the ark had its resting place on the top of the mountain between Steamer Point and Crater.

Here before me were the creatures, man and beast, bird and reptile, amphibian and mammal, and man was but one of many species.

In pairs made He them; He gendered them out of clay, and in pairs saved He them.

Dancing two by two, they moved in a crowd, not in single file as they made out in Sunday School; their movements were bacchanalian, as in a Goan fiesta.

The opening to the Ark was a duct, coloured red, and the Ark itself was shaped like the camel-skin water bags water-selling Arabs carried on their backs on the desert waterfronts.

I rub my eyes, and the luminiscence of light fades; the street is empty of motion or sound except for the clod, click, clack of the one-legged Muslim beggar, out to sing the song of Ramzan to wake me and the faithful Muslim actor across the street. Every night in the season of fasting, his footsteps wake me into vision; I sit up and listen, for his sounds are both throaty and aimed at the blue beyond. The beggar has a wooden leg; his clothes flap around him, but his intoxicating voice, thrown high above telegraph pole and cloud, hits the notes of that very song I heard on desert minarets, calling the faithful to break the fast for the day. He comes every night.

Dreams are never as strange as what meets the eye when wide awake. Dreams have a system; they have structure, beginnings, middles, ends; their logic is the logic of all creation, because the dreamer is autonomous.

Man in his conscious images uses the logic and system of dreams.

There is a familiar metaphor in Indian philosophy, which when translated to reality is the image of mercury spilt from a common thermometer. It runs about touching everything, yet remains untouched. This is not an unattainable goal, it is very often the only possible means of survival.

The Indian myth is full of stories of how old men and women, nearing their geriatric end, take the youth of the child they produce in archetypal moments of snatching life. They do not sell their souls for wealth as Faustus did, but they snatch the youth of the child of their own loins.

Mother insists one night that I go and lie next to them in bed. And each parent has one hand on my head; thus touching a sacred object, they take one another, and in the ritual act take from me my youth, for in the dark the sounds they make are terrifying.

As I sit beside the creek, where the whirlpool of water under the bridge spins in circles down to the seascape, I see a calf trying to mount a cow. What is natural for animals, is reversed for the Indian. Any society that is old finds itself reversing all animal postures. This essentially is the Fall, the original sin.

I am lying on the sand at Golvad. The shore is infinite. I lie on the sand and shout at the top of my voice, "Spirit of Keats come enter into my body!" I want to be a poet; I want to write. But the sunsets of Golvad are so beyond words that I despair. Watching rain in a movie, I get the smell of wet earth; synaesthesia is part of a writer's pathology, but words cannot evoke it as movies can.

What fascinates me is the epitaph on Keats: HERE LIES ONE WHOSE NAME IS WRIT IN WATER. I shout, I beg, I roar, Spirit of Keats come enter into my body. Make me a poet. I must sing. Spirit of Keats come enter into my body.

"The girl is sex-starved; we must get her married," said R.C. above the din.

"She is ambitious and has imagination," said H.C. Mother is not happy if anyone praises me. She cannot tolerate it, if the praise is not from her.

Back in Bombay, our cook Aleyamma said to me, "Mirakutty, I want to have short hair like you, Mirakutty." She was on her knees.

When Mother and Father went for the races, she made me cut her hair. Aleyamma's hair comes down to her knees. In Kerala, a girl with short hair is worse than a widow in the marriage market; a girl with short hair trying to get a groom is about as natural as a nun in a convent advertising in the matrimonial columns.

I hacked at her massive growth of hair. She kept saying, "Mirakutty, it takes so long to dry, Mirakutty."

"Mirakutty, oil from it makes my white *chatta* brown, Mirakutty."

"Mirakutty, it gets knotted up if I don't dry it and comb it immediately, Mirakutty."

"Mirakutty, Mirakutty, Mirakutty, I get time to wash my hair only at midnight, Mirakutty."

One look at her and mother lets out a scream.

"Your mother Aleyamma. Your mother Aleyamma is going to be so angry with me. What am I going to do? How can I show my face in Kuttapuzha? They will say I made you into a man. Mira had no business cutting your hair. She is taking over everything. Who will marry you now?"

Round and round the house mother raved. H.C. was in the garage parking the car.

Aleyamma said not a word; she wept. Aleyamma was so overcome she maintained her silence; so did I, so did they. Till I left for school, no one spoke to me.

I keep to my rooms; I stand alone in the balcony. I study the footwear of people who pass every morning and evening by our house. Those who wear footwear are the regulars. They catch the same train every morning, and return by the clock; rain or shine they never miss a train. If anyone does, I make every attempt to understand why. I know, for example, when women who walk by menstruate. Their walk is different. I know pregnant women from the back of the body; they walk as if they are pushing a hand cart with their stomachs. I know when people's bladders are full; monsoon is the time for frequent micturition.

I once saw a barefooted woman standing at the bus stop as if nothing was happening, but a puddle collected under her. I went down the stairs and sidled up to her. I smiled in a friendly fashion, I looked at the puddle and at her face, and said to her, "What's the matter behen?" Behen means sister. "Since the birth of my many children, I cannot contain my urine," she said. There is only an eighth of an inch that separates the two different orifices. I touched her feet and wandered away.

I seem to have all the time in the world to lounge around, walk without purpose.

I see every morning a beautiful woman with very bad teeth grinning bravely at a tall man who hunches his shoulders, and his arms are loose-jointed like the arms of an ape. Faces begin to have general affiliations to species in the zoo. (My husband, Nanjundan, looks like a peregrine falcon, one of ten thousand species about to die out.)

The balance of weight of some women looks as if they could easily topple over. I get an idea that Brahmins walk differently from Shudras. A Parsi walks steadily, then stops, jerks or twitches, and then walks steadily again. From inbreeding, most Parsi men have bow legs. Gujaratis roll, and Maharashtrians walk with a spring to their step. South Indian women walk with their hands bent. If slim they watch their toes, if fat the curve of the stomach.

I read a great deal. With each exciting incident, I jump up and look at my face in the mirror, and return to the book only after I study my face in detail. In one romance, a man tells a woman she is beautiful, and she says, "You wouldn't think so if you saw me in the morning." I am baffled by this. I look at myself first thing in the morning and I think I never saw myself look better. In another book, a girl says to a man, "I want to be somewhere where there are no footprints." I feel I must go to silent cliffs and lonely places. I sit in the shadow of the Fort and look seaward.

Cousin Mathai passing through Bombay stops for a night at our flat. Mother and Father make him sleep in the balcony and lock all the rooms leading to my room. At night when I wake up, I find Cousin Mathai sitting on a chair at the head of my bed, and he is holding my hand in his hands. Terrified that R.C. might see him, I said, "Go, please, go back." It pleased me he had to test his nerve, walking through my parents' room and across the dining room to get to my room, and he would now have to retrace his way! And that is precisely what he did. It pleased me, particularly, as I had just finished reading *The Count of Monte Cristo*.

4

WHAT SAVED ME FROM COMPLETE ATROPHY WAS THE FACT that I joined Anand Bhawan, a working man's college for Harijans and lame ducks. I joined Anand to spite H.C., not out of a social conscience. I wished him dead. But since he did not oblige me, he cleared me of the death of Sister Casanti. It is not enough to wish someone dead. There is no magical power that resides in a wish. In Benares they say, for the price of a few annas they can, by the power of their minds, remove anyone you wish removed, even from the antipodes. But the men of Benares have been practising tapas for generations. Yet it gave me satisfaction to note that whenever a business friend asked H.C., "Where does Mira study?" a purple flush sufficient to clog the arteries appeared to choke him. If the convents were instituted to promote selflessness, Anand College was there to give deprived men (occasionally women) a sense of self. What it did to me was to teach me the limits of self.

Laxman, who ran a bidi shop next to Light of Asia, an Irani restaurant, asked me, pointing to the copy of the *Sunday Observer*, "Is that your personal copy?"

"Yes."

"Are you trying to show off?" Am I trying to show off? Why did I join Anand?

"Journals, Laxman, are for my old man what bidis are for you."

H.C. has become a writing machine. He is a freelance ghost writer. He sells his ideas to politicians who wish to persuade the masses. He translates the garbled messages of illiterate Arabs; he invents slogans, catchwords, jingles. He is the man behind other people's success. He sells politicians to the people. He is the missing link, the go-between. He has a foot in two different worlds, an entry into two sets of dreams. He has brains, but is fast becoming a pander, to himself unreal—a gimmick, contingent, absent yet present. A seller of dreams not his own, estranged, becoming a lie to himself.

A stern, dignified man, an irrational man, with his heart in the medical profession; a man who has never wept, never confessed, now gives way to tempers and savage silences. He smiles at potential clients, at newspaper celebrities, at brassy tycoons, but grimaces only at home. In public, his expression takes on that of a street corner beggar uncertain of the rain of coins in his direction. What is it that makes such a man put on a masquerade like this? A man must provide. But what does he provide? A kind of guilt gathers around me. Are children responsible for turning young men of vision into oily-palmed touts, to become the great providers?

I learn to walk barefoot, or with shoes that have holes in them; I wear the same sari—a mill-made cotton sari—day in and day out. Mother is the best dressed woman in the city.

The elite of Anand are exempt from classes. We contribute at another level; we edit, we debate, we put up mock parliaments; we educate ourselves sitting at the Irani restaurant, Light of Asia.

Light of Asia is our headquarters. The light here is murky from soot-covered naked bulbs; the windowless walls are full of Persian murals and mirrors; the waiters oblige us with an endless supply of tea, at ten naya paisa a cup; we pay when we can, for we have credit.

A new thing is on our minds: the map of India is truncated; at high school they taught us to draw the map free hand; at college we cannot recognise the outline of divided India unless its comes along with the mainlands of outer Mongolia and outer Siberia. We offend the Paks by calling them Indians.

The outlines are unfamiliar; all signposts have been reversed. Streets bearing familiar names now carry names difficult to remember or spell.

Clive prancing on a horse in the centre of the plaza, for a hundred years, turns overnight into Shivaji, also on horseback, not prancing, but coming down the Western Ghats.

"Soon, no one but Maharashtrians will have a place in the Light of Asia," says Sreenivasan. A little ahead of the rest of us, he goes through slums muttering, "This is the hour of the knife!"

I develop a new aesthetic; I say, "Beauty is stasis, boredom. Ugliness is energy. Asymmetry, not symmetry is the need of the day." Emerging from an orphanage, exorcised of Christianity, I become a blotting pad, like the greasy dust-cloth on the waiter's shoulders.

India, till now the last word on envelopes sent from foreign lands, that I, like schoolchildren the world over, strung in a chain of reference to reach from extra terrestrial outposts—Bombay, India, World, Universe—now seems dismembered, but the scissors and paste job done on the map was also done on us.

Our neighbour's neighbours are our friends, for he, our neighbour, is the common enemy.

Yet, when I look at the map and look at Kautilya's neat circles, I share the confusion of the Chinese in not knowing who is neighbour to whom, and who the enemy.

Ranjan is untouched by politics, by Partition, by the heads of communal groups rolling in the gutters. What blights him is his father's great wealth. Ranjan skipped college till he was too old to enrol as a regular student. He, like Laxman, wants to become a lawyer. Laxman has to climb. Ranjan has to make it on his own. Neither very exceptional, wishes to join the profession that once attracted Gandhi, Jinnah, Sarojini Naidu, Johannan, and every national hero. Born too late in time, they too hope to reach the top by retracing the steps of the last generation of heroes.

Indians too talk of the generation gap. They borrow phrases, but it is meaningless. At thirty, an Indian is still treated like a child of ten. On their deathbeds, Indian patriarchs and matriarchs send for their children and say to them in the voice of death, go and be happy my children—and they, children no more, are themselves as old as those rattling on the deathbeds. At that phase, what is the difference between a man of fifty-two and a man of seventy-two, I ask you. The group at Light of Asia was trying very hard to cut the umbilicus. Mine, I told them, was severed at age four. They don't believe me till they meet H.C. What is he to Hecuba, or Hecuba to him, I say.

Melvin was the brother of a painter living in Paris; his brother's canvases fetched figures that ran into thousands, and he lived off what his brother sent him. It was not the dabbler who was financing the artist here, but the artist financing the dabbler. A touch of originality about Mel.

He attended every church in the city to listen to church music. If Ranjan was fat and jolly, Mel was lean and jumpy. Both have a touch of the carnival about them. They sing songs, clown, play Gog and Magog.

Keki Battlibhoy was a Parsi merchant's son. His hooked Persian nose, red complexion and bowlegged jerkiness, apart from suggesting intensive in-breeding, also connected us with big business.

Ibrahim Kazi, a Muslim, had no parents but owned a building by the sea and a house on Colaba Causeway called The Loft, where we were always welcome. An old aunt lived with him, but no one ever saw her.

We meet at the Light of Asia every day. There was one difference between them and me. They were free. They could do anything. They could be out all night. Once, when my parents were out of town for a day, I went with them to Juhu at night.

I sat on the sand at Juhu. At the hour of midnight, an old man emerged out of the half-light to sell me turtle eggs.

The scene is a cold half-moon, the beach incandescent, luminiscent moontide speckled with phosphorus cat's eyes.

Natural lights of the sky illuminate clouds from dark to light, and light to dark. A wayward moon dips and rises beyond the clouds. The air a balm, a salve, takes possession of every cell.

My hair whipped by the breeze teases the scalp, no longer moist from the day's heat.

I draw finger marks in the sand, my body winds and unwinds, with the cloud, the moon, and the sky, the water now near, now far.

Crouching beside me is this old man saying, "Turtle eggs, turtle eggs make good soup."

His eyes, slit between furrowed brow and burrowed cheek, glint at me.

I cannot believe that he is real; he seems to have stepped out of dream-waking.

I lean forward and touch one of the eggs. It crinkles to the touch. In appearance like a ping pong ball, but soft.

It takes the imprint of my finger, but slowly returns to its round shape, the impression fading; the man disappears just as he appears.

I turn to the others and ask them, "Did you see the old man selling turtle eggs?"

"Which old man?"

They had seen no old man.

"You've got old men on your mind."

"What's the matter with you? Reading *Rasselas* once every six days, talking of telepathy and reincarnation. Be your age, girl!" said Ramnath.

Ramnath is uttering one of his long sentences: "To find a new road to socialism, out of the rubble of the past year, the Ninth Plenum of the Polish United Workers Party has adopted the social, political, and economic objectives laid down at the Eighth Plenum held last October when Wladislaw Gomulka was re-elected party leader…" It looked like he was writing an imaginary lead, talking to himself.

Charu is saying to Sreenivasan: "In a Gandhian country like India, planning should start with the preparation of village and district plans and those should be fitted on like a jigsaw to form the national plan." Sreenivasan seems to be raising the question: Is the plan top heavy? Is it over-centralised? Laxman's preoccupation: Is there an undue stress on heavy industries? Dadi: What about cooperative farms? I listen to them and learn that planning is a means, not an end, as most things are, and the low national income is the starting point of planning in India.

Isabel is lying on the sand.

Ranjan pulls me against his stomach, and to my alarm I hear his stomach go gleeeehaaaaoooow! Gleek, glooo, gleeeeak. I get up in alarm. Ranjan thinks I am overcome; thereafter he talks to me slowly and gently; I ignore the signals. Isabel says: "I wonder whether J. Krishnamurti is a phony!"

"Why does he avoid the company of other philosophers?" says Ranjan.

Ramnath pauses writing his imaginary lead and says: "Should a poet keep the company of poets?"

They ask him to tell them about J. Krishnamurti.

"He was once hailed as the Messiah. He is a remarkable-looking man. His voice comes from deep within him; he churns his thoughts out viscerally, chops his sentences up, rewinds, and rewords, each a skein, each repeated and illustrated, yet he is a spellbinder. He can negate time, significantly alter space. Experience, he says, lies beyond choices, beyond action, beyond memory, beyond thought, beyond words. The mind should not be cluttered up. Memory, like choices, is the result of man's alienation from the heart of matter. Choices are the result of confusion. Space and time, good and evil, are all illusions. Evolution means not only progression but regression too. You can become a lizard or skip ninety-eight lakhs of lives. It is all the same. To the eye at the centre, all things on the circumference are equidistant. Ultimately, there is no good, better, or best. No hierarchies or norms or reflexes of given norms. The man who sees an oak tree becomes the oak, a woman who sees a flower becomes the flower."

"Are those his words or yours?" Isabel asks Ramnath.

"His message lies really beyond words; he uses words to suggest the unsayable. I have heard him sitting under a tree, in Madras, Calcutta, Delhi. I have heard him for some fifteen years now. I mean to follow the talks this season. Ramakrishna has a parable about all this. A doll made of salt goes to experience the sea; immersed, becomes the sea and cannot return to tell you anything. All true experience lies beyond words."

"Isabel, don't you feel that the doll made of salt is the way women experience things? And for that precise reason must at all costs avoid the sea," I say.

"Perhaps, but as an actress I believe what Stanislavysky said, 'If an actor believes he is the character he plays, fire him!'"

Ramnath makes a ridiculous statement about the moment of composition. "There is the expectation of a white sheet of blank paper. I sit there shaking my pen," he says, pulling out his pen and making forward thrusts.

Ranjan says to us in a whisper, "I can see him shaking his thing at seventy."

Isabel says, "I saw the *Ramayana* on the stage today. Rama and Bharata had blue paint on their body, I wonder why."

"Blue is the colour of the gods in classical India; all avatars of Vishnu are blue. He is a cloud-dark god, probably belonged to the Dravidians before the Aryans came."

"Why was Bharata blue?"

"I don't know." For once Ramnath confessed he did not know something. The others looked at one another and grinned.

"Sita was buxom," continued Isabel, "and looked like any South Indian Brahmin housewife. The style of acting is that of a Tamil movie. There were two hundred and forty-four scenes, it seemed to me. Sivaji Ganeshan delivered a mile-long rhetorical line without pausing for breath. His exits are inimitable; walking on the spot, he struts and sways, looking at his audience over his shoulder. He knows he is king." Isabel pauses, and Ramnath asks her if she had seen any Tamil movies; Tamil is Ramnath's mother-tongue.

"Yes, I saw one; it crushed me; I felt a steamroller had gone over me. It expresses something I have seen in Hindu homes again and again. It could be that no one else saw what I saw in the movie; my ignorance of the language might be the reason why I feel so crushed by it."

"Tell us about it," he said.

"I think it was called *The First Born*, about a mother and two sons and a house built with the father's blood. The first half of the movie shifts from song to dance and dance to song; it is a kind of miscellaneous entertainment, but it ends at the intermission with the older son's marriage. It also establishes the wife as a mere shadow of the mother. The wife flits about, looking pale. Enter the villain and his mistress. The plot begins. The villain is connected with a garage the brothers own, which supports them. The movie now transforms the first born into an Oedipal figure. He takes on the mistress of the villain, squanders astronomical sums of rupees, and slowly destroys, bit-by-bit, 'the house built with the father's blood.' The younger brother now becomes the Great Provider, obviously the father figure, the man ignored by the mother. The infidelity of the first born does not break the wife's heart but breaks the heart of the mother. At this point, the younger brother's mercy is infinite; he extricates his brother each time the mother pleads for her first born. Finally, the younger son, one day, brings the brother home in a drunken coma. At this point, the wife comes to life for a brief moment. Then when she needs the presence of the other two the most, she shrieks out, 'You! The two of you have beaten him up! You, mother and son, get out!'

"The mother considers this a betrayal greater than the liaison with the mistress. The younger son is at last enraged. He cannot forgive his brother, decides he will provide no more. Final crisis is the death scene; the first born is dying. He asks for his brother; he wants his brother to forgive him. But the brother refuses to appear. The mother does. But seeing he is dying, she falls across his body, and dies. The wife stands at the foot of the bed; the younger brother now arrives and stands next to the young widow. In his hands he is carrying his dead brother's child. The last shot before fade-out has the picture of the mother and the first born garlanded with marigold, side by side on the wall. The wife dressed in white, clearly still a virgin figure, looks at the photograph on the wall with a strange look of recognition and detachment. The younger son, still the Great Provider, holds in his arms his brother's child. He too looks at the picture on the wall. The camera holds them thus for a long moment. The movie started as a musical comedy. For sometime no one, neither actors nor the director, seemed to know which way it would go."

Looking at the audience as they came out chattering and laughing, Isabel wondered whether she had imagined the whole thing. She felt so totally and completely crushed by the unintentioned nakedness of the movie.

As Isabel fell silent, everyone else did too.

Ramnath confessed that he was the eldest son, and though he did not take to drink, he had never really cut the umbilical cord.

The Christian, the Parsi, and the Muslim decided that for them their fathers were powerful ideals, and the Hindus, Laxman, Charu, Sreenivasan and Ramnath said that they could never feel any resentment against their father because their fathers were so unreal; they merely provided the money, and were never seen except at the morning and evening meals.

"Talking of parents," said Melvin, "if you go to Mira's house, you get the broom in your face." I do not know if he really did go to my house. But Laxman, Ramnath and Charu did. I was not at home, and on my return found them standing at the door where they had been made to wait. I told them I would leave the proofs of the manifestoes at Kazi's the next day, as it was vacation time during Diwali and we did not meet at the Light. Laxman said in a loud voice, "Take care! You are in for it!"

As soon as they left, H.C., who was in his swivel chair, spun around and said, "They don't respect you. If they did, would that man have said that!" he spat out angrily. "You go to study, not to hobnob with the pavement dwellers of Bombay."

"They come from better backgrounds than most people I know."

"Don't tell me that! That man runs a bidi shop at Flora Fountain!"

"I am going to start one of my own some day," I said.

H.C. shot out of his chair and slapped me on my face. But that was all he could do. If he prevented me from going to college, I could always move out, and take a job like the others and live like them. I had done well for myself in joining Anand. Mother meantime decided I needed more leisure and she kept me isolated at my desk. She said, she herself has never been to college.

When I was in the Junior, Sreenivasan said, one opening day of term, that I should go with him to the chawls of Bombay.

He took me on a gutter inspection of Bombay. That day my eyes were truly opened to the true tapestry of India. I felt the water in my mouth turn to salt. We went through the chawls of Sewri; we stopped in the back alleys of Matunga and Dadar, and visited the cabins made of rags floating in the marshes. We stopped by every beggar, every bootless cadaver.

A man stooped and picked a leathery object from the garbage bin and washed it in the gutter and ate it greedily. Salt in my mouth, involuntary spasms in my stomach....

There were hordes of lepers. I watched one. Holes for eyes. Face cretinous. No gleam in his eye. Not human.

A mass of rotting flesh. Sleeps on a cart pulled by hand by his keeper—the woman who pulled no doubt for someone else's profit. She had no blouse; her nipples were discoloured, and hung at the end of a long and narrow pair of breasts. I found it hard to give them any money, though I had my lunch money with me. They should be at the leper colony. The thugs who exploit the sick should be boiled in oil, drowned neck deep in vats of boiling oil.

Seeing I was turned inside out by this experience, Sreenivasan set me a task. He asked me to write some articles for a syndicate he had started.

He said, "It's not enough to say I will follow Gandhi and clean lavatories. We have drama troupes, we have poets, journalists; we use anything we can to bring about change. The responsibility is ours. We are merely employing your talents." He did not give me much choice; he thrust into my hand a police file on a freedom fighter and asked me to write an article.

I sat up all night; pored over the dots and dashes, and telegraphic coded information about the activities of a Black List Society, out of which I picked what I could, about one Arunachalam who terrorised the British in the Kolar Gold Fields in the early forties.

I have reproduced it below exactly as it was—it was published in translation in several languages, none of which I could read.

> During the Civil Disobedience Movement, the younger generation came to realise that they had to fight the British with guns and bombs. They typified, as young activists always do, the passions of the repressed and the downtrodden. It is true Mahatma Gandhi elevated the

freedom movement to a high moral crusade, but it was necessary to bring the struggle down to the level of the enemy. The British did violence at every level to the Indian spirit and the Indian flesh. Violence was justified since the entire nation was behind it. When one such young activist was condemned to be hanged, Pandit Nehru is reported to have said, "The memory of Bhagat Singh will always stand between us and the British Government."

By 1942, when the Quit India movement was well launched, and the country was resounding to cries of "Do or Die", there was a small band of terrorist freedom fighters in the Kolar Gold Fields called "The Black List Society". In August of that year, inspired by the speeches of Subhas Chandra Bose, a young man called Arunachalam, who is now a soft-spoken doctor in a hospital at Bangalore, formed a compact group of anarchists called The Black List Society. Besides Arunachalam, there were only 12 other members. According to their rules, no member was to be under any compulsion to remain in the society against his free will. But at the same time, penalty for any wilful leakage of the society's activities was to be death. Married men were not allowed to join up. If any loss of life was caused by any activity of a particular member, that member was to surrender to the police.

One morning, the Kolar Gold Fields woke to find every bit of available space on the walls and pavements smeared with the injunction: "Kill British". In the night, Arunachalam had gone about with a pail of paint, working on the English lettering. Others, Narayanaswamy Reddy, Suryakanthi Rao, Munirathna Reddy and Ethiraj wrote in Tamil. It changed the quietness of dawn the next morning. The police were out immediately with a divining rod; they started arresting all and sundry. General political awareness, usually nil in the K.G.F., now began to be the main thing on everybody's mind. Matters got to a good start when The Black List Society convincingly informed the magistrates that the police had rounded up the wrong birds.

As a preliminary to its terrorist activities one of the members, Parthasarathy, was entrusted with the task of blowing up electric posts. With his eyes crinkling up, Arunachalam says the first post wobbled this way and that, held by over-head wires.

One night soon after, The Black List Society ventured out in full force to blow up the Irudayapuram bridge, between Robertsonpet and Andersonpet. When they were all set, people began pouring in from a nearby picture house after a late show. The men crouched in the shadow of the bridge till the crowd reached a safe distance. Then in sight of everyone they lit the night with a terrific explosion.

Headmasters Jolted

When asked why the society was called The Black List Society, Arunachalam said that it was the purpose of the group to make a list of the anti-national elements around them. For instance, they thought that the headmasters of the K.G.F. schools were rather lukewarm in their nationalism. They decided to act. As Gandhiji's birthday approached, they sent intimidating letters to the headmasters saying that if they valued their lives they were to celebrate Gandhi Jayanti in the school premises. After the destruction of the Irudayapuram bridge, the magistrates advised the headmasters to start the Jayanti celebrations.

During this time, the present Chief Minister of Mysore, Mr Nijalingappa, was at the Champion Reefs Jail. When he heard of the society he sent a message to Arunachalam, offering them financial help. Arunachalam sent the following reply: "Dear Mr Nijalingappa, regret inability to meet you in jail. My mission is action, not exhibitionism. My coming and meeting you in jail will not be of any help to me because, though I appreciate your generosity in offering financial aid to this society, I am not in a position to accept it. I cannot accept financial help from someone and spend it on whatever *I* think fit ... I don't find any need to meet you at present. By the time this reaches you, you will hear of some shocking news. Yours faithfully, Leader, The Black List Society, K.G.F., 1942".

When the electric poles were blown off, some of Gandhi's men were arrested. After pointing out to the police that they were barking down the wrong alley, Arunachalam set out to drive the point home. The society planted bombs at 8 o'clock the following night, at four different places, simultaneously, at the Robertsonpet Police Station, the Andersonpet Jubilee Hall Talkies, the Skating Rink, and the Olympia Talkies. If there was any loss of life, the member responsible was to give himself up to the police, but nobody was killed that night.

Gandhiji believed all action was tainted and it must be admitted that a great many of those who took part in such violent activities were just a caboodle of profiteers and upstarts who left in their trail sabotage, arson, looting, and murder. Yet their violence gave British complacency a rude awakening. Some of them, like Arunachalam, infected by the injustices of the time, acted with courage and won a brief fame.

I thought for a while and gave it the following headlines:

TERROR IN K.G.F.
THE BLACK LIST SOCIETY OF 1942.

I read it again, felt it was a kind of routine job. I did not, I thought, exhort violence. But later when I looked at it, I found that I had placed Dr Arunachalam with Bhagat Singh. I did not see my article in print. I believed friends who said they saw it in Gujarati and Marathi.

Sreenivasan continued to give me work. One day, as I was returning home, I saw one of the Anand students throw a bomb into Joshi's car. When questioned he said, "I want to kill him, I want to kill him; he thinks he is the greatest poet alive; I hate him!" The poor, pajama-clad boy, Ajit, wrote poetry and hated the guts of his one-time idol.

H.C. heard of my political activities. I was leader of the Labour Party in college, spoke in the town hall at our mock-parliaments, wrote these articles, and was seen with Sreenivasan.

"What do you want to do when you finish your studies?" he asked me in his haughty fashion.

"I want to be a journalist," I said.

"Which woman is a famous journalist?" he said.

I mentioned Bapsi Kokdavala; it was the first name that came to my mind, and he said, "That woman! She is notorious! No decent person will ever be seen in public with her."

I did a little bit of research on Bapsi and found there was nothing wrong with her; there were people who suspected she was a lesbian and shaved regularly. (Japanese women shave their faces.) From then on, H.C. seemed to have only one goal for me—to become a teacher. I decided—that would be the last thing I would do. I told my friends that after the exams I would make a little bonfire of all my books and notes, and never enter a university as long as I lived.

A series of riots in Bombay, public acts of violence, looting shops and bombing public buildings, made me aware of the fact that sporadic acts of defiance and terrorism would benefit no one; it only made the Gandhi caps feel more righteous and sanctimonious. I began feeling uncomfortable about my contributions to Sreenivasan's syndicate. To make me realise that my part of it was almost negligible, he took me to see one of the plays they staged.

It was on the life of Napoleon. There are people like Laxman, who have read no other books with pleasure except biographies of Napoleon. Hitler and Mussolini have a tremendous following. Though I did not follow the dialogue, what amazes me is that the acting is so rugged, the stage effects startling. The play is in Hindi, conducted in a new theatre in Dadar T.T., but the professionalism of the production stuns me. Hindi movies are acted in namby-pamby fashion. The story line is an excuse for song and dance; the clown is as important as the action; the heroine when weeping always breaks into song; the hero swings his hips like a belly dancer, and ogles like a village idiot.

Here violence and action are one.

I needed to go to the women's room. At the door to the yard stood two strong women with arms like Hamida Banu, the famous woman wrestler. They pushed me into a corridor along with several other women. They expected me to offer resistance and relieve myself on their toes or on the inner lawn, the size of a diaper.

In the corridor I saw twelve pairs of buttocks, from pale to dark brown. Some of the women squatting there had pulled their saris up their waists.

The buttocks are not an unpleasant sight, a series of smooth, polished curves, but their squish-squish squeal rhythm is unnerving to me, who was feeling the pressure on my own bladder.

The lavatories stood empty. I go into one of them, and shut the door. I cannot shut out the sounds, but manage to pull down my panties without incontinence. My own sound seems mediocre and muffled.

When I come out, I see another twelve pairs of buttocks. No one seems to be wearing panties. Perhaps this accounts for the fact that there is no unpleasant odour except that of ammonia.

I learnt a great deal about the new India from the play, and a lot more about the old India from a visit to the women's room.

Rachel David at Mount Mary's told me a Jewish joke about how the Hebrew-speaking Jew from Baghdad, visiting her grandmother, used the ploy of muffling the sounds by turning on the tap. Rachel's grandmother snorted to everyone's embarrassment, "She pisses like a horse!"

I remember an English friend of H.C.'s remarking on the high IQ of some Indian children and boasting, "I always tell Margaret, 'Margaret, all our bodily functions are the same.'" And I said to him, "Dear Mr Smith, you can easily say that of your cat Sheba too!"

Needless to say I have never been popular with the Smiths. But Rachel's father was different. Being a rabbi, he came to the slaughterhouse to bless the meat. We used to scale down walls, and down the steep incline of Mount Mary's hillside, past two bazaars and the railway station to see this fat, jolly patriarch. He brought us goodies we could not get in the school tuck shop. The nuns never found out. The price of being adult is that one would not risk all for a lemonade and doughnut. The taste buds of teenagers have more pleasure than anything in adult life.

There is a Mr David for every Mr Smith, social scientists please note. But Sreenivasan is a theorist, a dogma-ridden activist. I think of the individual instance, but Sreenivasan speaks of mankind, from China to Peru.

As a test of Sreenivasan's good sense, I submitted a news clipping to him from a Delhi newspaper. It was about a man whose father, grandfather, and great-grandfather before him were ivory-carvers. His father's work was in the Bombay museum, and his grandfather's in the Salar Jung museum. Now old himself, his eyesight failing, he decided to create a work that would be a fitting farewell to his craft, both on his own behalf and on behalf of his ancestors. He mortgaged his land and house, and for six years worked on maunds of ivory. He worked day and night and created a man-sized ivory lamp, carved fine as Belgian lace; he worked into the tracery birds and animals of every kind. When he finished, he had nothing left except his lamp. He sent it to the All India Handicrafts show. He asked them not to use a high intensity bulb. He won the first prize—ten thousand rupees. It had cost him one hundred thousand rupees for just the ivory. Three months later when he went to collect it, he found that they had left it under a tree, under a mat, with a high intensity bulb which they forget to turn off. The ivory was cracked by heat and stained by rain water. The museums were no longer interested. He had offers from foreigners, but he did not want the piece to leave the country. He was willing to settle for half of what he had spent, if only he could get one of the Indian museums to buy it!

Sreenivasan threw the clipping out. Cake instead of bread? he shouted. He had the goods of the world divided into necessities and luxuries, and Indians according to him should forget their peacocks and ivory, and think of the man rinsing out pieces of garbage in the gutter. Everyone got terribly hot over this argument, but I felt there was something terribly wrong and terribly right about Sreenivasan's position. Yet, it was no different from the American view of India: the best Americans say to Indians, "You, who have seen poverty and disease, who daily see the dead and the dying, you must behave better than us, have more of a conscience."

This does not make sense to me. The gilt may not be gold, but in India the poor man's wedding glitters as much as that of the rich man. Both rich and poor share a common mythology, common festivals. Every Indian is at heart a princeling. Every Indian woman, old or young, poor or rich, well or ill, has a princess complex. All you levellers, all you westernised reformers, you cannot change the Indian dream. And what do you know about it? Consider this—the rich man can forget ivory and peacock quicker than a poor man can.

Of course, Sreenivasan does not like being told that he is a westernised zealot. We argue. I tell him that there is no difference between me and my maid Phullora. We are very alike. And as for the students at Anand, they may be called Harijans but they were no different from the Brahmin Charu, or the Brahmin Sreenivasan.

In any case I cannot think of mankind from China to Peru, I can only see what I see, feel what I feel.

Melvin goes to church just to hear Bach. He sits for hours there. To him it does not matter that I went to pieces when I saw an epileptic get a seizure outside my gate. I watched the man frothing and groaning outside the gate. His fingers clench this way and that, twist around each other like roots of ancient trees washed and eroded by rain and sand. His dhoti doubles back exposing his balls; they too are polished black and gleam in the hot sun. I watch helplessly, unable to move.

A crowd soon collects.

One man, a tall man with hollow cheeks and high cheek bones, wearing a striped shirt and crumpled dhoti, asks the girl standing on a wall next to ours to get a piece of iron.

The girl who lives in the servant's quarters walks back along the wall, runs on it, her long skirt and braids flying around her. She hops off and is back on the wall. Her agility is typical of the poor young of Bombay. As they get older, they lose this careless grace and speed.

In her hand gleams a butcher's knife, the blade several inches thick—the only piece of iron she could find in a hurry.

My head spins; the sun blinds me; I can see the butcher's knife flashing in the hand of the epileptic and doing a good job of hacking. The tall man waves away the girl in the long skirt. His shadow in the noonday sun is pigmy, and his long, slender hands corded with muscle and vein, wave the girl away.

"Pani lao!" He calls for water.

"Piaj," says a woman standing near me, asking for an onion.

A passerby on a cycle flings down a bunch of keys on an enormous key ring, big enough to go round the epileptic's neck.

The keys are pressed into his hand; miraculously he stops foaming at the mouth. He continues to groan, but opens his eyes.

Men famous in history, men I had read of in my studies in literature, men like Mohammad, Caesar, Dostoevsky, Maupassant come to mind.

What was the difference between those epileptics and this naked beggar, I wondered.

The moment before and the moment after, pre and post as in coitus, or in moments of vision! The seat of memory and recall in the brain is seized by a staccato of electric waves, spikes, and flashing pictures in the brain, along with strange powers of foresight, premonition, and *déjà vu*.

The man continues to groan. The moment after is always different from the moment before, as in pre-menstrual and post-partum. The clock of anyone about to fall, and the intensity of the moment is not that of merely feeling the sun or the emptiness of the stomach (this man's stomach seems to touch his backbone as he lies in the sun), or the gleam of the button on my purse, shining in the sun, but that this earth must be to this man as full as it is for me. Despite the alpha, the beta, the theta or the delta of his brain waves, he too sees sky, and tendrils of grass shooting up, rocks browning and rocks green by the waterfront, and that passion that poets feel of the crystal clarity of what is, things beyond pleasure and pain, even of good and evil. That moment before the fall, this man foaming on the sidewalk was a king among the gods.

I called our maid, Phullora. She serves as translator. The nuns did not teach me Hindi; they taught me French. She says, he says; it's like a bilingual liturgy with its echo:

I am four and a half rupees away from home.

I am four and a half rupees away from home.

I am going to a hospital.

I am going to a hospital.

I was travelling without a ticket.

I was travelling without a ticket.

I am going to the G.T. hospital.

I am going to the G.T. hospital.

When the conductor turned me out, I lost my sense of direction.

When the conductor turned me out, I lost my sense of direction.

I felt fear.

I felt fear.

The sun is very hot.

The sun is very hot.

I know suffering is my karma.

I know suffering is my karma.

Even shame.

Even shame.

I ran in, and took five rupees from my mother's purse. Sufficient for him to go to the hospital and back. I regret I did not do more. But I have nothing of my own, and even if I had, would I? Is not a lot of my feeling and observation momentary? This thought gnawed me. I felt hollow and phony, and wished there was a cause I could give myself to, absolutely without a tremor of doubt.

To keep my sanity too, I told myself, I have to be tough. Practice toughness. What haunts me is the look in the man's eye. The frightful intelligence of the man. The next day when I meet the group, I am still full of it.

"He was human; his eyes gleamed. They recognised me as human too; they thanked me, but he said nothing; his eyes gleamed."

"So, it was not the man, but the gleam in his eye that haunts you!" Habib, being Muslim, felt the epileptic was a brother, and if at Habib's door, would have drunk out of his own glass. All Muslims regardless of class share the same cup, as in Aden. Mother once pointed out that Muslims everywhere were carriers of all the deadly diseases under the sun.

"No. What I mean is that he is not merely human and my equal. He is my superior."

"Individuals don't count," said Sreenivasan, "if we stop to help every individual we meet, we won't get much done. The woman who said, if I can't have a millionaire let me have a million men with a rupee each, is a nit. Even if she met them in a line, thirty a day, it would take her three thousand years to get down the line...."

Behind my chatter was a pendulum of alternatives. I should have done more for him. I could not have done more for him. If I gave all, I would be declared mad. H.C. would be the first to get me certified. Or I would be walking the street. Not having been raised on the street, they would put me away. One of my phobias is that I may be turned out of doors in the summer months, and that I might have to stand in the sun at noon and die of a sunstroke.

"The only way to be sane," said Keki, "is to think of oneself, one's needs, goals." Are goal-directed people sane? Do they do the greatest good? Parsis maintain schools for the poor Parsis, sanatoriums for the sick, and resthouses for the aged. This is because the Parsi entrepreneur is not ashamed to advance himself, make something out of nothing, amass a fortune, and set aside enough for the needy. There is not a single Parsi child who is deprived of school or medical attention.

"Above all," said Ranjan, till now narcoleptic like the dormouse, "worship money like my old man. It will buy anyone a return ticket from hell."

"Crave for sex. Tell every male or female you meet, with a turn of the lip and droop of the eye, that you are ready like the earth itself. Sex appeal is the secret of success. For me, all the good things in life are free, like listening to Bach at the Cathedral. My brother is an artist. He creates, he provides. The principle of life, Sreenivasan, is based on consumption, not organisation."

Ramnath, arbitrator par excellence, raised a stubby pointer and nostrils full of overgrown hair hard to look at; he said, "That, Melvin, is the American way. Your brother's market may be the American tourist. They want to take home a picture of what Christ on the cross looked to an Indian. It does not matter to them that the artist is a Goan, raised in England. The principle of life Indian style is conservation. Each Hindu who belongs to the world has Mammon as God. To some extent the mystics of any community point out that society's greatest flaw. If material things mean a lot to Indians, the sadhu or sanyasi will have nothing but his begging bowl. He is the contra to everything. In the rest of the world, even in the west, it is no different from here. In the ghettoes of the world, hungers beyond words roam and foam and scream, unprotected by police, or self-discipline."

"What bothers me," I said, "is that when I feel for the epileptic, I am not sure I am quite sane."

"What are you talking about?" asked Isabel who had turned up dressed in a salwar kameez. "We are talking about beggars," said Habib.

"Talking of beggars, an old woman turned up at our flat the other day. Wait till you hear of this one," said Isabel. She deposited her khadi shoulder bag and books on an empty chair. Isabel is our Renoir girl with black hair. She wears the same mysterious wondering expression as in a Renoir canvas. Her lower jaw is full. She has good skin (nourished by the glycerine of hormones), an eighteen inch waist, and her lack of pigmentation contrasts with her black hair in a startling, eye-arresting manner. Her internal world is a mystery to me. I don't know about the men, but I certainly find her mind-filling. Isabel's mother-tongue is Portuguese; she speaks in English to us, a language she learnt outside her home.

Isabel was saying, "Her hair was wispy and grey; a knot loosely tied on top of her head left the hair loosely framed around her toothless, aged head."

As I listened to Isabel, the thought occurred to me that, unlike old Mrs Skinner or middle-aged Mrs Smith whose Caucasian skin had taken the gnarled parchment of skin broiled by the sun, old women in India recalled grandmother and romantic thoughts, old age ruminative on a verandah with thoughts of a turbulent past, wordless and far away. And I a child, standing by her, would play with her earlobes that once had borne too much gold and now had a lobe through which I could put in three of my little fingers, a slender loop of ear cartilage, and knowing her quiet unawareness of my presence I would know that her thoughts were full and resonant.

Isabel said, "This beggar woman's blouse-front sagged, her breasts peeped through, long, thin, and unfettered. She sized me up. She knew, the crafty old witch, that I had a problem about her. Actually, what I was thinking was how good she would look on stage. I set my jaw tight against her, but she knew my eyes found her irresistible and fascinating. She would not take no. She had to have something. Anything. She would not go away. She went from window to window. She seemed to take possession of the yard. She lay seige. Then, seeing she was not getting anything, her whole aspect changed. She straightened up, and in her leanness grew in stature, no longer benign but a righteous Kali. Her hair flew. Her stick, long and knobby like her arms, rose; she waved it. Her toothless lilac, ridges flashed momentarily; her lips snarled. And she said in Konkani—I was surprised she was Goan—'You will pay for this. In three months when I return this way, there will be a big lock on this house. They won't have to carry you very far. You live in the right place. Muslims go that way. Hindus go this way, and you Christians are right down this way over that wall, and Parsis of course have to be taken up the hill; birds eat *them* up.'

"She was dead right, we do live very close to the cemeteries and the crematorium in Charni Road. My mother was getting very nervous; she wanted to give the old woman anything and everything she possessed. As you know, my father is old and my mother is not quite herself. The old hag knew this; so I forbade my mother from giving her anything. 'You will be dead in three months.' Why three? I wonder."

Ramnath said, "It is not for nothing there is a trinity; there is the sun, moon, and stars, and think of Tom, Dick, and Harry."

"Ram," said Isabel, "do you think it would be a good idea to gather some of these beggars and let them work out a play? They could act in their own clothes, and we could supervise their roles, but they could let their fantasy run. First we could take them to see some of the *jatras* (popular Bengali folk theatre form) that Sreenivasan is arranging, and then we could have a play by the beggars."

"A beggar's opera? It's been used by Brecht, you know," said Sreenivasan.

"I did not mean that, using them as characters for a theme. No, a real live thing, they could more or less play as they want, and we can let them take us where they can, and let it be a kind of real life play."

No one really thought that Isabel was serious, but she was, with rather macabre consequences for all of us.

My contact with the group at the Light of Asia made me take an interest in Phullora. I found on talking to her that she was a very morbid woman. She loved collecting florid stories and each story she told bore the stamp of her personality; I was never sure that she did not make it all up. I could not talk to her while my parents were at home, but when they went for a late show or party, Phullora would come and sit on the floor and she had in me an ideal listener.

Her real name *was* Phullora; her people belonged originally to Bihar. Her nose was pierced on the wrong side since she was born in a scavenger family, but to confound the world she got the other side of her nose pierced too. When she was young, her family had converted to Catholicism.

She prefaced most of her remarks with the words: "It was in the papers."

She was illiterate, and most of her vocabulary and gestures came from watching Hindi and Tamil and Bengali movies. After each movie one had a hard time deciding which region she came from. So aptly did she mimic the lifestyles of these films. She also had the knack of a seasoned storyteller; she would preface each tale with general remarks about the nature of the human condition. As now, when she began saying: "Miss Sahib, the children of the rich too are lost in strange circumstances. A corrupt contractor built a luxury hotel of mirrors that rose into the sky but was built with sand instead of brick and mortar, and it fell on top of a rich Sindhi's child going out to buy sweets with me, but I escaped unhurt."

But Phullora's mother, big with child, paid her price to placate God. She went to the lavatory and the child fell into it and was smothered by shit. Missahib has no idea what the lavatories of the poor are like, she tells me, making me feel here is a lot I do not know.

Phullora herself owed her mother undying loyalty. She can never forget the fact that her mother lost her left breast trying to feed Phullora.

How on earth did that happen?

Breast-feeding is the same for the poor as well as the rich. To quote Mr John Smith, "All our bodily functions are the same."

"Well, there was not much milk in her breast; so she tore her nipples with her fingers thinking that that would bring milk out, but instead of milk there was blood."

"Her breast got septic and had to be removed."

When her mother died, she made Phullora swear on the Bible that she, Phullora, would never marry. "This world is full of illusions Missahib, and men are a very bad lot."

It was written in the papers, she said, but she watched it with her own eyes. There was this thatched hut near the creek. She herself did not live in a thatched hut, because they are liable to go up in smoke.

She pays fifty rupees rent, but when it rained, a whole wall collapsed but no one was hurt.

"In this thatched hut were all these men, women and children, and some cows. The stomachs of the cows burst like bombs—boom, boom, they exploded! And those men kept rushing into the burning hut to save their gold and silver, their women's jewellery. As if gold and silver are more precious than lives! When we die we cannot take it with us, can we? These Hindus are very cruel to the dead, that is why we became Christian. There are enough trials in life, without our torturing a person after he is dead. They burn their dead, and when the body stands up in the flames, they hit it with a stick.

"Missahib, you are so beautiful, better than a film star. I have worked for some film stars, but they are not beautiful. Their faces are all burnt under the paint from standing under big electric lights.

"But my mother, she was beautiful—she had a nose like yours. A long nose. My nose is flat, my eyes are narrow; everyone tells me I look like a Japanese, except that I am black."

I could not bear her story about the torn breast and the asphyxiated foetus.

I lay down in bed and felt my head about to explode.

My nipples were frozen with pain over the idea that anyone would possibly tear it or puncture it like a rubber nipple. I found myself running up a temperature; I think I was delirious all night.

Tall ashok trees, stately, aloof, soothe the spirits, swaying like magical vines, doing a rope trick over the gates of St Xavier's College. In the outskirts of the city, still pools and gutters of rain breed mosquitoes. In the evening light, a man with filaria slowly walked past me with the gait of an elephant. He wore a pair of khaki pants with buckles on them. How could Sanskrit poets have compared the walk of a beautiful woman with that of an elephant?

Occasionally, the memory of the man picking offal and washing it in the gutter and eating it, turns my saliva into salt and I feel like retching. At mealtimes my mouth gets flooded with salt. I talk to Phullora about it. She says that no one need eat out of garbage, even hotels give away free food if you go there, but there are people who do not relish anything that is not out of the garbage. She says, at wedding feasts in the south, where she worked, when they throw out the banana leaves on which food is served for the guests, pariah dogs, mongrels with sores and flies, and crows fight with these men who grab it from the dog and beat the crow to it because they relish offal, she says.

They chose the beggars off the streets; they picked them for character, though they chose them as one does fish or fowl or pet in the market—one for his teeth and hair, another for his bawdiness, a third for her vocabulary. They then took them for the *jatras*. They gave them the idea of the play. One of the men, lean man with a couple of strands of hair for beard, seemed to understand, take command, take orders, give orders. Isabel supervised; Sreenivasan supervised; they had a part mime, part spoken, part bhangra (a Punjabi folk dance), and wound it around the theme of the country mouse and the town mouse, as most of the beggars had some knowledge of what it was like in the village. The family in the country got its script right. But in the house of the town mouse, showing a street fight, the man with the goat's beard (who till now seemed to understand everything fully), took out of his belt a real knife and stabbed his adversary to death on the stage. He seemed very proud of his act. Watching the plays on Hitler and Napoleon he had got the idea that those who fell on the stage were truly dead. The police were there, as Isabel had permission from the Commissioner for the performance. But it shook us to the very roots.

When I got home that day, I went to bed without dinner, but it was Phullora's day for further macabre reports. Nothing could silence her, except the kind of act I had just witnessed on the stage. So I let her report. "Nowadays they give money to the men if they allow the doctor to operate on them, so they won't have children. My boyfriend wanted some money. He went to the government clinic; they gave him thirty rupees. But Missahib, he has become a eunuch."

"That's a lot of nonsense; he will be all right in a few days," I told her. But she had much more to tell.

"When I got my pay this month, I sold my nose-jewel and with it and my pay I went to the municipality to buy the land where my mother is buried. If you pay the municipality sixty-five rupees, you get half the actual grave, and I paid for a slab with her name on it. It is not the full size of the grave, but half. But I asked the man who was digging the place to put in the slab, to dig deeper. I wanted to see my mother again. He said the police would get him. So I bribed him to dig deeper. I gave him ten rupees. He dug quickly.

"O Missahib, they have been telling us lies till now. My neighbour said if you touch a dead body, the devil will get you. But there is no devil; I am not afraid of the devil or God anymore. They told us lies. They told us that we would all rise again and be with God." She drew in her cheeks, exposed her teeth and gums, pointed into her eyes signifying empty sockets and said, sobbing, "That's how she looked! Even the hair, bits of it crumpled like ash in my hands. My neighbours told me the devil will get me. But no devil will get me. Mother will never go to heaven or hell; she is finished, gone, and as for me, I am going to get married as soon as my boyfriend recovers." I pretended to sleep. But decided that sleep was impossible, as soon as she left.

The next day we found out that the man with the goat beard had escaped months earlier from thana (the Indian word for police station), and that he was not illiterate. He came from a lower middle class Muslim family; his name was Faiz. Which did not bring the dead beggar to life, but explained something to us. Beggars in the street have at some time watched Ramlila, seen Ganpati, and some fifty other festivals full of ritual and drama where no real blood is ever shed in enacting either epic or folklore. So they could not have pleaded ignorance of something acted out as distinct from something lived. Hanuman did not walk the streets, but he was there in every other street performance.

We went for the cremation of Bhai-Bhai, the dead beggar. I have never before gone for a cremation. I continued to sit under the shade of the trees, outside the crematorium in Charni Road. The procession of the dead passed me. Summer corpses punctuated the day, with ritual and song and dance, more studied than any I had ever seen on stage. There must have been a seasonal thing going, something of epidemic scale; I could not imagine that the number and variety of the dead that day was typical of every day in the year. I followed one carefully, the clanging of cymbals, the smoke from the sacred ember, the silent crowd, barefooted, an occasional sound of funeral elegy or song. This must have been a Brahmin. (Dances in front of the bier signified the low caste; the size of the bier the wealth of the dead.) Brahmins had more austere funerals. Funerals of babies swathed in white. A black gilt-edged coffin came on a Victoria, with horse and bells, the coffin sticking out like a tall man on a short bed. I walked on, into a side street, towards Grant Road.

Beyond the railway station was the bazaar. Always at moments of stress, it was fun to walk through crowded streets; they were never to be exhausted; one identified them with the olfactory nerves. Booths here displayed plastic goods, in pinks and incredible greens, strangely inartistic. More so when the skyline showed in any other city, granite in black of temple tops built by whole generations, epochs earlier. Only Bombay lacked them. Bombay had other wonders.

There were always the hawkers and the gawkers; masses and masses doused in sweat spilling over into gutters and onto streets going two ways. A new definition of brotherhood comes to mind: breathing nose to nose, not shoulder to shoulder.

Two aspects of Bombay shock the Malayali. One, the day's litter, and two, the awkwardness of seeing Indian men in western clothes. Coolies in kurtas look fancier than babus in bush shirts. Here and there there were a few redheads. Was it henna or lack of protein? The bearded in this part of the city were clearly Muslim.

Occasionally there were faces with turmeric applied on them as a cure for any skin problem.

Near the market, in a narrow alley, on a windowsill that looks like a niche, sits a naked man with manic joy in his eyes.

At the end of the alley, a child, a boy of five, has on his lap a girl, a few months old, naked, sleeping as if blessed by angelic hosts, and with the flush of sleep on her cheeks. The boy eats a stale piece of bread, crumbs of which fall on the infant's Mount of Venus. He picks up the crumbs and eats them greedily.

Next to them is a glossy, prosperous cow, chewing a poster off the mossy wall.

At the bus stop, a man and his son get off. The man has a neatly folded off-white sheet on his shoulder. Between buses, he goes to the tap by the bus stop kiosk and washes the sheet. They get a hold of the ends, and twist it into a rope. The wet sheet now looks mud-coloured. They open it out, turning it this way and that to catch the sunlight. Slowly, dry white patches appear on the cloth; the patches begin to spread; the whole sheet is dry. The father folds it neatly and slings it on his shoulder, like a vendor of fabrics. The bus comes; they find standing room on the foot board, and ride off towards Mahalakshmi.

BOOK TWO

I

LUCID MOMENT WITH NANJUNDAN. LUCID BECAUSE illuminating. Nunjundan's ideal is that of a Hindu mystic, mine that of a Christian. We are husband and wife. His name is Nanjundan; I call him the Mahatma.

When high he brays out, "Now I understand everything. Your Christianity and my Hinduism."

I return from an early morning walk and find him in a coma.

I don't know what! Could be codeine, or morphine, or mescaline. Could be hashish, marijuana or opium or just plain alcohol. Or it could be just nothing, a mystical state.

I drag him to the bathroom, tickle his throat, pour ice-cold water on him. I drag him to the sofa in the front room. I rub his body; his head keeps rolling off the sofa. I pick it up, a dead weight, and when I place it on the sofa, it rolls off again and falls on the floor at my feet.

I try to force coffee down his throat and he brays: "Coffee, caffeine, drugs! Nobody gave me coffee the day I was born!" He lies still and brays out again: "Now I understand everything. Your Christianity and my Hinduism."

He goes at it alternately.

Nanjundan is lean and dark. The corners of his mouth go up in a permanent curve even when he cries. His nostrils are so fine that you can see through them as through the walls of some fine Mughal tombs, where through marble so finely wrought one can see sunrise and sunset. When he sits still his hands and feet or the corners of his lips are in constant motion. The tendons of his neck have their own convulsive rhythm, as now when he lies naked as the day he was born, and cries out for mammary glands.

The sunlight through the window falls in a crazy quilt, chequerboard design of dark and light. The evergreen of pines outside the window lets in the light in angles that meet and cross.

We are in the Himalayas, the Abode of Snow, at a station called Khilgesh several hours up on the blue train from Simla.

The only thing that puts Khilgesh on the map is the International Writers' Farm at which we live. We are part of an experiment in international living. A superior publicist could have thought of no better guinea pigs for experiments in a lifestyle. Writers not only live but publicise. We are also excellent sponges. We absorb, we record, we sift, we regurgitate, we vomit, and we return to our vomit—not merely to sniff but to describe.

Each of us who lives here has leased the land for ninety-nine years for the cost of less than it takes to rent a boat on the Dal Lake for a honeymoon. What I mean to suggest is that the whole enterprise is a joke, and the laugh is on us, prisoners of our own delusions. Khilgesh is the collective dream that every one of us once dreamt individually; and so the foreign capital poured into this place had no trouble collecting us.

Nanjundan and I go over the heart of the matter. For Nanjundan the Mahatma, there is no individual soul, only the collective, the All. He is not just a man; at the highest moment he is also a woman.

Ramakrishna in his moments of ecstasy actually menstruated.

The first time I showed Nanjundan a soiled menstrual napkin, he passed out. Nanjundan desires both men and women. This does not prevent him from approximating and appropriating my femininity.

But I am a hole. A woman is a hole. Nanjundan's identity reaches sainthood when he makes me sit in front of him, naked, and our two organs meeting, resting against each other, he says:

"Is that my cunt?" and I shudder.

"Is that your cock?" he says and I shudder again.

It is a mystical moment for him and for me just plain crazy.

Now that I am living with a Hindu Brahmin, I feel that every inch of me is me, territory I know by heart. Every inch of space around me is my space; every moment of experience is mine.

But Nanjundan invades my privacy, appropriates me as him, and makes out he is me.

In Nagercoil, where he comes from, the bathroom is called a bathhouse. There is no bedroom but a bedhouse. Anything with a wall is a house, not a room; there are no doors; a shut door means you are shutting someone out. A closed room is inspect; all doors are kept open.

If there is the vaguest suggestion of privacy, it is between the family and the outside world. All members of one family make a unit. At the same time, the name for father—Ayya in Tamil—is used along with any other name when inclusive, and the word for mother—Amma—is added to every woman's name if she is known to you. She too is included, so that the family unit is not just father, mother, child, but anyone and everyone within the area of inclusiveness.

This means that the idea of a room of one's own is an alien idea.

For me, the three a.m.'s of my mind are my own. My room is an inviolable space I carry always; to touch and be touched is to permit the outside entry through a high gate and a moat over which stand sentinel time and experience and memory and conscience and consciousness. A part of me, because of my Kerala background, is familiar with the Hindu.

But there was the attic, the tree, the river, all mine. There was my God, and the people in the sky put there by me.

To Nanjundan, for whom there are three thousand given gods and goddesses and Brahma who is really himself too the centre of the circle and the circle itself, the imprint of my hand on the smoky window, placed there in pain, is the imprint of the hand of a goddess. He stares at it for days.

Nanjundan returns from a trip to the Institute for Advanced Study at Simla, where he had gone to take part in a conference of astrologers. They needed his services as a statistician needs a computer. I don't tell him that. If

I do, he would shrug and say, "What's wrong with that? The human brain can never be as good as a machine."

I don't think he really believes that. I don't know what Nanjundan really believes. I can only record what I hear, what I see.

Nanjundan arrives early in the morning after calling me strangely the previous night. His voice on the phone is flat and chatty. Watch out, watch out Mira, I said to myself. Something is the matter.

I avoid him all day by going into the woods and staying out of sight.

In the evening he puts away the dishes for me. Everything is meticulously put away in its place on open shelves. His concentration on each item of crockery and cutlery mesmerises me. I sit there in the kitchen watching him. I can wash things but I can never put them away in place. Down below in Simla, Delhi, Madras, Calcutta or anywhere in the plains and hills below us, neither of us would have to do such chores. There would be a Phullora or Aleyamma or a widowed aunt to do the work. But here at Khilgesh we are trying out a new life, without servants or widowed aunts. I can wash things but I can never put things away. Carefully laundered clothes are carelessly flung into drawers out of sight, and I have some four hundred saris that Rahel sent me, most of which I never take out because I find it hard to put them away in place.

"I meant to tell you, Mira," said Nanjundan, pausing between the wooden dish rack and the cabinet above it, "but it slipped my mind. When I was dining with Rao yesterday he said something interesting. The only interesting thing he said in fact. He said that Peter Bradstreet was working in his office when the roof collapsed. They suspect some foul play and blame the Naxalites, but it may have been an accident; they are investigating it. His face is mutilated, but he is fully conscious. He has lost an eye and part of his nose, and one side of his face is partially crushed."

Nanjundan's voice is quiet and chatty.

"Where's Kavita?" I said.

"Kavita?" he echoed, his voice going up.

"Yes, Kavita," I said, my throat burning like acid.

"You mean Kavita Dayal?"

"Yes, yes. That's who I mean, Kavita Dayal."

"Someone told me that she and her husband are in the Pondicherry ashram for the year." He says the words hurriedly, as if such knowledge would imply further knowledge which he wanted just as hurriedly to deny.

Really workedup now, but controlled, I say, "How shall I describe Peter? What's the word? He was a consumer; he had a gargantuan appetite for life. He took passion and pride in himself. He was not self-preserving, or he would not have gone after a girl like Kavita. But I felt somehow that he could afford it. He was built on a different scale from others."

It occurred to me suddenly that Nanjundan does preserve himself. For a man who has attempted suicide repeatedly, he has kept Kavita engaged in harmless games, compared to what happened between her and my friend Gopal, between her and the obstreperous American writer Peter Bradstreet who now lies in the hospital with his face crushed.

I saw Peter Bradstreet—a tall, broad-shouldered man with a clear milk-fed complexion and firm jaw and clear-cut features one associates with pictures of astronauts—at Mrs Peabody's. She was then my landlady.

Mrs Peabody is a missionary at heart, but a secular one. She is at Khilgesh, she insists, to provide the refinements so lacking in a backward country.

She flapped around Peter in wig and slippers. Her presence distracted me. But I noticed that Peter's Anglo-Saxon cool did not hide the fact that he was studying me as if I was a notorious deviant and he a psychologist. I did not understand that scrutiny then. I do now. Peter's manner is both careful and careless, and for a moment I am thrown off-centre, my breathing uneven.

"Why did Kavita try to commit suicide last December? And why is she at the ashram?" I asked Nanjundan.

"How do I know?" He sounded impatient, which is unusual—as if I were setting traps for him.

He has completed his task. For a man who has spent his life shaking a pen, Nanjundan shows infinite capacity for change. He never makes the same mistake twice. His computer has a supernatural retrieval system. But life itself has an even greater range of permutation so that each time a new area throws up another feature of strife, he will—as if doomed to do so—do the one thing that is least expected of him.

His room-mate, Alfred Anderson, once in a charitable mood, described Nanjundan by saying, "Nanjundan's one goal in life is to confound and confuse the other."

We are still in the kitchen. When I want to avoid his eyes I keep glancing at the batik painting on the kitchen wall. I am aware of the fact that ever since I heard of Kavita's suicide attempt, she comes to my mind often. I do not mention this to the Mahatma.

I hear a monkey's excited gibberish on my back verandah. I have grown accustomed to these semi-humans. But the screen dooris always latched. The one occasion it was not latched, the male, the female, and a brood of monkey babes had a pillow fight and the fuzz from the cotton in the pillows remained on Nanjundan's hair for a whole month. They also made off with Nanjundan's Afghan cap.

Nanjundan leaves suicide notes in the bathroom cabinet, in my dresser, in a little wallet in his raincoat; but suicide for me is not the ultimate freedom but the ultimate in the obscene. He seems to know full well that the suicides of old companions have gone through me like knife wounds.

Phullora was found hanging from the toilet chain that comes down from the ceiling. Her eyes were shut like one saying prayers, though I knew she ceased praying when she dug up her mother's grave, an exhumation that robbed her of every belief.

Habib lost an eye in a car accident, and during a game of bridge, he excused himself, went into the next room and shot the roof of his head off.

Charu took pills, wandered to the phosphorous-lit waves of Juhu, was found dead on the sand, his prominent teeth grinning at the palms overhead.

There were also the ritual suicides of friends rich as Ali Pasha, who out of weariness bathed—perfumed their orifices—scattered towels and silks across the floor, so that their steps from the bathroom to the canopied beds would not pollute their ritual cleanliness, to die deaths as delicate as Cleopatra.

Or those mistaking Camus' intention in *The Stranger/ The Outsider*, activated chains of suicides from Cape Comorin to Khilgesh, and in this lighted keg, some were found in gardens tended by obedient malis.

Rahel, hearing of this, wanted to read *The Stranger*. Alarmed, I burnt the book in the kitchen sink, like a Baptist parent anxious about the spiritual health of his offspring. I could not bear to have Rahel's great charges of vibrancy defiled by such wantwit sadness. Consequently, she withdrew to her rooms for a day and emerged saying: Mira thinks I have no brains; in my father's house I read a lot; in Calicut, while I was carrying Mira, I read Dickens.

And Nanjundan. Nanjundan is a man without a past.

Paradoxically, he can see himself in five incarnations. He spent some years with a rishi in the Himalayas. Man of many callings, many professions. I have heard well-known men claim Nanjundan as a fellow botanist, biologist, artist, musician, philosopher, historian, satirist, and mathematician. I suspect he has three or four MAs. He has written an encyclopedic outline of the social sciences. He hopes to complete the whole series for a time capsule. The man's entire life revolves around being all things to all men. As it is, he divides his time between the Institute for Advanced Study and Khilgesh. Why would such a man want to kill himself?

I have many questions to ask Nanjundan, but if I do, I would behave just like him. He is always asking me questions.

Why are you smiling?

What is that frown for? And so on.

I am full of questions myself today. Why does Kavita, though married, insist that she is a virgin? Why has Peter's wife shaved off her hair? Why was Enid Bradstreet so fearful and tearful about meeting me?

She would not visit us, and refused to come to our party. She cried on the phone, excusing herself. But she praised Kavita to me. Kavita was at that time sporting Peter around as her latest conquest. When Kavita visits them, she wears Peter's shirts at night—or so Kavita informed me.

I met Enid at the Mall. A tall, angular woman with high cheekbones and a manner as if she had spent her youth in wartime Germany. She was dressed in slacks. A black scarf over her square, shaven head made her look like a novitiate in a convent. She waved a bunch of coriander leaves in my face and said they were grown in her garden for her by Kavita; she was taking a few leaves over for Mrs Peabody. I could have told Enid that coriander grown in the backyard brings bad luck, or so Phullora used to swear.

Kavita is a well-known Punjabi-Bengali playwright. Her parents settled in Bengal. Recently, her first film, *A Touch of Sun*, was dubbed into fourteen languages and shown at a film festival in Delhi. She has long limbs and a full figure. Her hair comes down to her knees. When she first arrived at the Farm, she used to put on eyeshadow and sit in front of the mirror in my room, practicing how to look seductive.

At that time we were both boarders at Mrs Peabody's.

Miriam—a visiting Lebanese-American drama enthusiast—was coaching her at the time on how to look seductive, and they would come to my room to practice the art of amorous isometrics.

When I looked bored, Kavita flattered me by hinting I was an authority on such matters. When I looked offended, she hinted that Miriam the Lebanese girl thought so.

Kavita at that time had a complex about her small breasts. She used to stuff handkerchiefs into a size D maidenform.

Kavita continued to practice in front of the mirror; she would wet her lips, twitch her facial muscles—and it seemed to me that she looked as if someone was torturing her at her other extremity. But her efforts at sex appeal were not wasted, as events proved later.

Kavita's father ran away with his son's wife and the mother took to reading the *Grantha Sahib* the days when she wasn't fasting. Kavita said that by fasting her mother did not mean a meal a day. She would not accept even a glass of water.

"I had to be understanding. I had to understand Pitaji and Mataji. What about me?" she said, not forgetting the isometrics.

I had no answer to that. Yes, what about her?

Kavita's mother is two generations removed from her, and somewhere in the background.

She said to me: I never really related to my mother.

She was an idea.

A point of belief.

I hardly knew my father, and what I know I'd like to forget.

In her teens, Kavita fell in love with a neighbour's husband. She referred to him as "Jyoti, the famous Bengali architect". I have looked up the *Who's Who* and could find no Jyoti who is a famous architect—one of Kavita's fabrications no doubt.

Kavita was always torn between the idea of what she described as being like her father and being like her mother.

By the time she came to Khilgesh and met Miriam, it dawned on her that there was a third possibility—being herself. She was not quite sure what this meant; hence the various rehearsals, the isometrics.

Nanjundan and I both know her individually. Nanjundan met her in the Viceregal Palace in Simla during a weekend of meditations. They both share one feature. They act as if rumours are ideas, and ideas facts. She sought Nanjundan out, even asked him later to write her a love-letter, a literary one.

He complied. He can do almost anything, especially when commanded to. She took the letter to Jyoti Sen, the famous architect, and twisted his arm by telling everyone that Nanjundan, the satirist, was beside himself courting her.

On the way back to Calcutta, she travelled to Delhi with Nanjundan. I have heard both their versions of the train journey to Delhi. With much care I reproduce what I retain of it: She undoes her hair. Shakes her head so that her hair falls around her, as in a Japanese movie. The train winds downhill. Lights glint everywhere. The train goes through several of the hundred odd tunnels, comes out into pitching hillsides, settles now and again to winding round the hilltops. Sitting down, Kavita's hair is down to her ankles. She gets up and walks across to Nanjundan's seat. He sits, applauding with his toes, smiling and grimacing at the dark mountains.

She says to him, "Any girl marrying you, Nanjundan, must have a sense of humour."

His lips continue to grimace and smile; the corners go up further and he says: "To marry me, she must have a sense of humour."

Her hair down, it mingles for a moment with his hair, and brushing her body against his, she said to him above the clatter of wheel and engine: "When you go to bed tonight, think of me." With a shy glance, her eyelids quivering up and down, she vanishes down the train.

At Khilgesh, a centre for an Experiment in International Living, I meet Nanjundan for the first time, when he comes to see Kavita. She is out with Gopal. She has just stolen him from me.

I ask Nanjundan whether he would like to step into the hallway since it is raining outside. He is stooping and looks as if he has no neck; at other times I have seen his neck look like that of a giraffe. It telescopes like that of a turtle. His eyes are large. He is hairy; there is hair all over him. He looks distraught, not from the rain outside, but something like the rain.

"Would you like to take shelter for a while?"

"Ouuu-nooouuu," he replied.

Man of few words?

And he dashed into the rain. Later he told me that as soon as he laid eyes on me, he saw diapers drying in the sun.

I have shown these pages to Nanjundan.

I tell him a figure of salt must forever avoid the sea. Men can sail the seas in search of white whales; they can hang up their souls at the Cape of Good Hope and pick them up on the way back. Men live sequentially; thing leads to thing.

Not for her. If she reaches the sea by instinct, as do newly hatched sea turtles, she will become the sea. The rest is silence or children.

If she is to talk, her words are like water to a sea of mackerel. Her story cannot be told with the "he said" and "she said" exclusively.

She cannot force a moment to its crisis. She is acted upon as when wine goes through water.

Pour her in any vessel and she will take that shape; run her through any terrain and she takes on the odour and grit of her surroundings. She carries the smells.

She is the chameleon poets want to become when they wish to be androgynous. She has no beginning, middle, or end.

She is an onion. Peel her if you wish to, peel by peel, and what do you think will be at the centre? Some tears! She is the goose that lays the golden egg.

She is a hole to be filled. Time and space and action belong to the triangle of space every man must carve for himself. But she is a paradigm. Her image is that of a crystal where every part replicates the whole. She is parabolic, repetitive, seasonal.

Nanjundan says, quoting Blake: "One rule for the Ox and the Lion is tyranny." His maxillary muscles move as if he is chewing a sweet paan.

Nanjundan wants to be the figure of salt. He wants to eat it, dissolve it on his tongue till he too is made of it. He wants to experience everything, even menstruation.

This distorts me. For I then get displaced. I leave the world of woman and become part male. But my time is my time. Not his. If not, I become a wild cat. I have my own territorial imperatives.

There is a carved chest in my room that I keep locked. He breaks open the lock and discovers there is nothing it. It is empty. There are various languages of communication, aren't there?

A prefiguration in a dream and I disregard it. All nightmares start in the familiar world. Awake, I lose the dream. What I reproduce are its ghostly remnants. (My dreams are uncertain about colour, what about yours ?)

A man comes to see him. They go into the study. The man leaves. Familiar things follow, a tabla somewhere on another hilltop beats a rhythm that is pure Karnatak. My pulse keeps the tempo of the drumbeat. In the nightmare waking I see a lean man in white, hairy, his face muscles in constant motion—he grows leaner and taller—he is nine feet tall and is about to have to bend over backwards to accommodate the roof. He stands there growing.

Who is the catalyst, who? Who is the doppelganger to whom? Nanjundan to Kavita, Kavita to me, Nanjundan to Gopal, Gopal to me. In patterns of doubles, sometimes trebling, variety multiplied in a wilderness of mirrors reflecting mirror images. But he stands there taller than tall. I AM TERRIFIED.

The Mahatma says to me: "Mira, you mustn't think that I am trying to make you cry; believe me, I am not trying to make you cry by telling you about Peter Bradstreet."

"Nanjundan, you have not crossed my mind; I am crying for Kavita. She has gone through life collecting problems. It is a full-time occupation. Now this terrible accident will crush her, that is if she is still human. Her lover is rotting in a hospital. She herself told me that he is her lover. And if she does not feel this accident, how will her husband be able to look her in the face again?"

As I speak Nanjundan's face changes; it changes into something indescribable. It shines with light. His eyes are full of an unbearable intensity. "Tiger, Tiger, my mistake. I thought that you were William Blake!"

"What is happening to you?" I asked him.

"I am depressed these days, nothing is happening to me."

"What I see is not depression but emotion," I said.

"I have to work; I have a lot of work to do," he said, and dashed out of the kitchen, hitting his shin against a step ladder. Later in the evening he goes to pieces.

"Nobody understands me! Nobody loves me! I will give up the struggle—what's the point of it!"

I can see him working up to one of those spurts of violence against the self.

I slap him on his face. I hold his head. I need someone to slap my face and hold my hands. A hand to soothe my brow. Nanjundan does that later. But much later.

Nanjundan says: "I squirm whenever I think of it. Nina is the most eligible girl on the Farm and engaged to me; I take her to a store in Delhi where I buy her a ten rupee ring on sale. I get it for three rupees. I even said to the salesman, it is for our engagement, Nina gets a headache; she stops talking to me. When we made up again, we lived in a flat in Safdarjung for a fortnight.

"She says to me, I know I can help you but why should I?

"Instead, she insists we go to the Medical Institute. They found there was nothing wrong with either of us."

"Nanjundan, why don't you go and see Nina? There are ways of looking at these things. Go see Miss Fang Tooth."

"Don't call her Miss Fang Tooth! She is lovely, very lovely, lovely in her bones, to her bones." He ruminates on this for a moment, grinning and grimacing, like a man chewing paan. "I will go on my own steam, not yours!" He leaps out of bed, busily knocks down the bedside lamp, picks it up, and waving it says, "You are always pushing me; why do I get pushed around?"

I go through a catechism; do I push people? Why do I do that?

My agitation reaches its height when he drops the lamp and bounds back into bed; trying to embrace me, he says: "Oh, I am glad you are pushing me." I feel as cold as a leg of lamb.

Nina has always been there these many years, with her signature of closely chopped orange rind. Every time I went to see Nanjundan, there was a heap of carefully chopped orange rind. I don't know whose presence leaves this tell-tale confetti.

But Nanjundan's room-mate Alfred Anderson enlightens me. Alfred's beard is speckled like the colours of an autumn wood in his native Ann Arbor, Michigan. He has the lean and supple looks of an Elizabethan courtier. Alfred enjoys telling me: "That orange peel on the dining table is Nina's work."

Alfred wants to tell me this. I stare at him. My mind is at the same time on this confetti of undigested feelings, bright outside and cracked underneath, cut into minute little strips.

When I met Nina, she looked like a cat that has had too much cream. Her face glows with the thought: "Look at this genius, I rejected him." It is written all over her. Her manner when with me is a trifle too vivacious. I see through it.

If Nanjundan's human function is to make women feel a sense of triumph, he has more than adequately fulfilled his task.

I have met this look on Sunni's face and on the face of the other woman whose name I do not know and will never know. They have all jilted him. In fact, Nanjundan is the most jilted man in modern India. In earlier times, the problem would not have arisen. A girl was affianced in infancy, married at puberty, given a large dowry, and thereafter the two families—the girl's and the boy's—considered themselves united in wedlock.

Nanjundan says to me, "I have no memories of Nina," and I am satisfied. I did not realise he could have said that of anyone. He has no memories of a childhood. He is a man without a past, and therefore the future ceases to count. His every act is an act of desperation, or of mimicry.

He goes on, "She is very unreal to me. We never really touched one another. She did not give me time to feel her. She said to me, 'Nanjundan, you can have as much of me or as little of me as you want.' And then she rushed me into taking her."

"Did not her remark seem to you a desperate one?" I asked him.

"No, why should she be desperate? She has everything; she has fame, friends, family, money, experience."

"Precisely for that reason. Didn't she strike you as unstable? A European girl from an aristocratic background would have to be pretty strange to catch hold of the first brown stranger in a foreign land and accost him with a proposition. Sounds to me like suicide." I used my one bad word.

"Why do you belittle me? You think loving me is suicide. You reduce me to nothing."

"Perhaps I do, but why don't you go see her?"

"You are like a detective, hunting me in the name of justice."

"Nanjundan, something is terribly wrong. You want me to be one, don't you? Is that my function?"

After that I decided to be quiet for a while. I have been talking too much. It shocks me that I should still be talking to Nanjundan. That I talk to him is a symptom of my condition.

But he will not let me be. He follows me around, asking, "What are you thinking Mira? What is on your mind? Why are you smiling? What is that frown? Talk to me!"

He cannot breathe. Sometimes this breathing difficulty continues for eight months at a stretch. At times it looks like he would explode from lack of oxygen. Hollow chested, bent over, doubled up, crawling about, as if breathing his last, he cries, "Nobody loves me. Nobody cares for me."

The only way he can get relief is by lying down. He will not lie down unless I do.

We have been together in white hospital rooms. They do a bronchoscopy on him at Ludhiana. He is under pentathol and takes time to come out of it. They give him oxygen. I am taken to the intensive care unit next to the operating room, and hear his throat rattling. I think it is the death rattle. Grandfather's brow bound in silk, his brow pencilled by blue veins. My dead dog—his bulging eyes fixed on a tongue held out for breath.... I come out into the golden valley of the Punjab with the sun glinting on wheat fields open to the sky; there is a great distance between me and everything. A haze. Far away, I can see the landscape on the edge of Ludhiana—wheat fields leading to other wheat fields. But without Nanjundan the world is empty. I stand there like one who has no substance, breath or being.

I go back. He says when he comes round, "I feel guilty."

"I feel guilty."

"I have made you suffer, Mira."

This shocks me as if he had really died. Who is the Hindu and who the Christian? For years my search has found a blank. There are words for shame, for crime, for failure, but none for guilt in the Indian languages.

Yet, can one parcel out guilt and responsibility like rations during the war?

The doctors can find nothing wrong with him. They are envious of his health. Though these frugal missionary souls are envious of Nanjundan's adolescent body, they declare he is the healthiest man they have examined.

Back home, a storm continues to brew between us.

"Caffeine, coffee, drugs, nobody gave me coffee the day I was born!"

Nanjundan confesses to me his fantasies. Then he wants me to turn into a watchdog and stand guard over him. The moment he met Kavita and Peter Bradstreet together, he decided to borrow my view of the world. He no longer registers the world except through my eyes. This puts an intolerable burden on me. He even thinks my past is his past. He has no memory other than my memory.

"Your problems, dear Nanjundan, are your problems." I used to think that human beings had central dogmas and creeds evolved because of the richness of human history. But now I know that the checks and double-checks are inside myself.

The truth serum can find in the depths of a Hindu mind as much guilt as in that of a Jew or Christian.

"I am no policeman; don't turn me into one. I am no breast-feeding type...."

Hindu India is full of breasts. Look at the sculpture. The base of each breast is large and round like the earth itself. The diameter of these perfect circles matches in width the base of the Mount of Venus. It is no use pulling at the breasts if the base is narrow, as the girls did in the Franciscan convent; if the base is narrow, you end up with a single long udder like that of a cow.

"What are you thinking, Mira!"

What am I thinking? What you want to hear is more about yourself. You also want to know why I am still involved with you. I once told a man that I would rather have a dog than him, and he said, "Maybe you will end up with one." Perhaps I will. Perhaps I will.

When I met you, you shuffled around. Often you would lie in bed till sundown. You never brushed your teeth. You sat in cafes all evening. You said to the waitress, "Bring me anything you wish."

You ate things that turned your stomach. But you ate them. You said to me, "I don't like to own anything. I can drift."

Everything was equidistant. Anything was possible, even murder. You kept groaning in your sleep, "Hai Ram, hai Guru, I am no worm in dung!"

I saw you and your remarks as a conditioned reflex, from the dark centre of our brilliant era. I saw you, and your problems were connected to larger issues. I said to you, "I cannot think of you as my lover, but as someone infinitely human. Others gloss over things, the real puzzles." But I got trapped. I have a halter round my neck. I have a keeper.

If that creep, Nayyar, had not attacked me at the Mall, you would not come upon me weeping. You took me to your room for a cup of coffee. You were so righteously angry. You paced about angrily. But what did you do next? You knelt at my feet, like a tired and sick animal.

We could not consummate the act for another half year. You would not believe me that I was a virgin. In fact, what you said was, "I am only half a man now. At any other time in my life I would not be like this."

Next morning, when your phone call woke me up, I said, "Last evening was a mistake."

"If you think so, we will leave it at that," you said.

"On the way to Aiyer's fiction workshop under the oak, we met by chance on the outskirts of the woods. I shuddered. Your shawl (cloak? loose cloak?) flapped around you. Your face was unwashed. Your hair dishevelled. Hair from your nostrils stuck out. I shuddered and the words "Gothic monster" came to mind.

I spoke of this to Peter Bradstreet months later, and he said, "Young women sometimes feel that way the first time they are taken."

In the women's romances I read, the heroes always had a club foot or a broken nose, Gothic defects at the sight of which the women fell like shot pigeons. I myself, when drawing into strange cities by train at twilight, when the lights began to glint here and there, and the figures in the dark hurried homeward toward the houses lit in the distance, have wondered if he, the man in my future, might not be one of them.

But you don't want to hear about that. You want to hear more about yourself. About us.

Two weeks later you stood once more in my path. You were kind, polite; you made all other men look like beasts.

You have two faces. I see that other face. I reprimand myself. You said, "Come have coffee with me; just to say that everything is all right between us."

Over coffee in your kitchen, I notice the pile of orange peel. You are talking to me about American novels, because I had started reading some for the first time in my life. You spoke of the open road, sea, river, the river of initiation, the open sea down to the whiteness of the South Pole; you spoke of that long road of motels. Then of the house, houses with seven gables, doors, of claustrophobic entombments...a dill pickle in a barrel turning out to be a dead kitten...I am impressed, I look at you keenly and catching my eyes, you stop and explode: "Don't look at me like that—you are asking for trouble!"

I did not know then what I know now. You can talk of anything. Your head has a computer. It has a retrieval system that has cross-references. You can spin across continents, across time; you have at the same time an imagination that focuses on particulars, on the detail, objects seen, tactile, visual, so your retrieval system hits the other as a felt thing. What hits the ear is passion.

But you are a mathematician at heart. You leave one thing out, the human, the heart—you leave the centre out.

That day I am held spellbound. Since then I have seen them—Lebanese, Japanese, Nepalese; Arabs, Jews, Indians—sit around you at midnight. When glasses tinkle in smoky rooms, as your eyes register the cleavage of breasts and the collage of hairless white legs leaning towards your Hindu hands, you produce from one corner of your brain those thoughts that give you a reputation for brilliance. Yet, you neither can sit backwards nor forwards when glasses tinkle—for it is so far from the *agraharam* that raised you. I know that you are "pinned and wriggling" inside, but you are also captive of that damned promiscuous intelligence. But I am spellbound by that trapeze act of daredevil assurance. You can do better than Bradstreet or Aiyer. You can talk physics to the physicist, you can talk with knowledge of beauty tips, and how to avoid crow's feet.

But I am not asking for trouble; I drop my eyes. My ears burn.

Your voice on the phone: "Is that you Mira?

"I thought of killing myself this morning.

"But I assure you I haven't.

"Want to see me now?

"I am wearing a cotton picker's hat that Enid Bradstreet brought for me from the States.

"A woman I know thinks I look like a secret agent.

"I said, yes, I am on a mission in search of myself."

I am patient with you at such times.

For the people on the Farm tell me that the whole town is sighing for you. They say you have

palpitations
fibrillations
insomnia, that you are taking
tranquilisers
goats' milk
and neem juice,
that you are suffering
pining

eating your insides out
because Nina jilted you.

Other women have rejected you, but they did not get famous that way. Kavita too has the spotlight turned on her everywhere she goes. For example, she has convinced everyone that she has jilted Nanjundan. There are moments of reverie when I think that perhaps all these women who claim they have jilted Nanjundan were in fact jilted by him, just as Kavita was. But Kavita is an unusual girl. I would be surprised to find more of Kavita's sort.

Sreenivasan had taught me a lesson sitting at the cafe by the shore in Bombay. He said, "Don't take what people say as scripture; at least consider the possibility that the opposite might be true." Sreeni was trying to teach me doublethink. But I must have my intrinsic defences. If I do not believe, I will go round the bend.

Doubt makes me ill.

When I doubt I feel nausea. I can only see, feel, act when I say yes. When I affirm I am I, you are you, and the world is, and all and everything is, is, is, always and forever, now as then and evermore. Amen.

I say yes, and then I dilate; then I fly.

Let the heavens rejoice and let the earth be glad. Let the sea roar and the fullness thereof. Let the fields be joyful and all that is therein; then shall all the trees and woods rejoice. Let the sea roar and the fullness thereof and the world and they that dwell therein. Let the floods clap their hands; let the hills be joyful together....

Nanjundan, there is no other truth than the felt thing. No books can give it to you, no systems of thought. It is an evasion. All you writers and intellectuals, burying yourself under dusty volumes and spidery notes, who listen with others listening to others. Writing dead words, reading dead words, thinking derived thoughts, regurgitating your second-hand hand-me-downs from other lives. You lost underworld of pen pushers, how you make me rage. Pale, vacillating, transparent without substance, without feelings, without corpuscle and skin, forever playing solitaire with faecal cosmologies. What is food for one is faeces for another.

I forget you want to hear about yourself.

Has it ever occurred to you that you are living by proxy?

You are trying to be me. Why? You have more prizes than I; you have arrived. You say this is a result of meeting Kavita and Peter. Why? What has that rigmarole to do with me?

Now you are appropriating me. Approximating me. A book I read is a book you have read. Anything I think is what you have thought. When I experience a landscape, you say it is what you have experienced. A painting I buy is a painting you have bought.

We met in that many-coloured August wood on the foothills of the Himalayas. You said to me savagely, "Don't gush like a schoolgirl!"

After that I was all yours. Incarceration and entombment, that was my need. I am a freak of nature; when they made me they left something out. I feel too much. I needed a keeper who called the lines. I put this halter round my neck. But even as with Lucky and Pozzo, who leads whom? The servant or the master?

Where was I? Oh yes. The whole town sighed for you in unison; they bled for this southern Brahmin pining away for this heartless White woman. They knew the score. About this white blonde, even they who sighed knew that this was as it should be.

There is a little racial estrangement in all of us. In Rahel, Nina, Mira, Nanjundan. How else can you explain away that three rupee ring?

Don't we all know that Brahmin Nanjundan has only eaten on silver and that mother wears only diamonds and silk? Now widowed, mother wears as befits a widow no diamond or silk, but does she not still eat out of sterling silver and use only ritually pure things, untouched by polluted sources?

And Nina is as straight as a pine staff.

You clever manipulator, you who manipulate me, don't you know you met your match in Kavita? She still had genuine feelings when she arrived here, but she also has a fervid mind. Fecund with the convoluted machinations that embroiled everyone for miles around her.

Yes, you smile when you think of her. And if I smile, it is because I know you got paid in your own currency.

When I met her on arrival, she said to me, "Poor Nanjundan, he is suffering."

"Who is Nanjundan?" I said.

"Don't you know? His father died in jail fighting for the freedom movement. Nanjundan's satirical articles and cartoons have become collector's items. In fact, nowadays I grab all his first drafts. Some day they will be very valuable."

"You can't be serious!"

"Perhaps. But it depresses me to see him.

"Why? Is he a creep?"

"Hardly. But he has been jilted, over and over again."

"Yes, I heard about that."

"Nanjundan used to write letters to me in Simla. In fact, my family were very jealous of this Brahmin from the south who dedicated his books to me."

"Then Kavita, why don't you comfort him, as only a woman can." She made a shocked face. As I looked up, I saw I think a fleeting combination of shame and delight. I misread her expression.

"Such women don't grow on trees," I added hastily. I thought, maybe she subscribes to the popular Indian myth that no man loved truly more than once. A heart once jilted stays splintered till the cobwebs of that love hide it forever from view.

Though a humorist, Nanjundan's ideal is to be like a child; if one toy is taken away, another seems as entrancing!

"Only the most sophisticated," he said, "can be like that." To be a child again one has to be sophisticated!

2

It is raining. I stay in my room. It is one of my rules never to own umbrella or mackintosh. It never rained in Aden. In Kuttapuzha water is as natural to the skin as air, and one could always protect oneself by holding a giant banana leaf or woven palm frond over one's head. A human being seldom learns anything after such. When it rained in Kuttapuzha we went under the bed. We were innocent then in our make-believe adult gestures of warmth. But rain always connotes splendour between the sheets. No sound is as musical as the patter of rain on thatched roofs, and waterfalls down the eaves of low roofs.

The landlady, Mrs Peabody, is flapping downstairs in wig and thongs. She collects everything from old hose to string. She has a haystack of discarded hose; this I call nostalgia. Indians don't wear hosiery, for static electricity makes saris climb up to the neck. But Mrs Peabody is clinging to a lifestyle she has apparently rejected by settling down in India. Nonetheless, she is a collector of more than old hose. Her cellar smells of rotting potatoes, stuff from the farm. She bought everything off-season; she lived under the notion that India too had seasonal sales like in Kansas. Unlike Indians who use their fridges only for cooling water, she stores everything in her fridge shipped out from Kansas. She even stores last year's snowballs. I have yet to experience my first snow. I once sent her a cake and she served me a slice from it six months later, and it returned as salt saliva for another six months in me.

The doorbell rings. Mrs Peabody keeps a doll's house. Everything is blown glass. Frills for the still and painted wallpaper, all washable. Toilet paper is rationed, but she insists everyone use it. Indians would much rather wash themselves. She will not permit the use of a shower. She insists on a tub bath for all her lodgers. With the result that most of them run up and down the hill looking for bathrooms with showers. Mrs Peabody is out to reform Indians.

The girl in the room next to mine is not Indian. She is Chinese, from the mainland. Her name is Foo Yang. She cooks all day. I think of her later when Nanjundan makes me cook round the clock for months. No sooner have I finished one meal he brings another crowd to be fed. But Foo Yang who walks as if she has an invisible child strapped on her back, cooks with a dedication that is rare. She sings, as she cooks, such sonorous hymns as *Take it to the Lord in Prayer.* She dates Nayyar whom no one else will date. He has a swagger now. When Nayyar first arrived here, he was naive. He gave an English girl an LP record and next day he saw her having coffee with another man; he rushed up to her and wailed aloud, "Give me back my record!" and they laughed in his face.

After that his skin got oilier and his glance more calculated. He grew a beard. On the first night out with a girl, he would show her his bed. He did not want to leave things for the morrow. No Indian girl will be seen with him. But Foo Yang sings hymns.

I come down the stairs to answer the doorbell. It is Nanjundan at the door. I am smoking a cigarette and he stares at it. He tells me later that he had never seen an Indian woman smoke before. His hair is wet. He has no neck. Cold and clammy, something envelopes him. I see a large red heart ticking into enormous arteries and veins connecting it back, red and blue—the diastole and systole of grief. I had no idea then that he has hair on his chest. An important matter; H.C. has no hair on his chest.

Idiculla refuses to be seen without an undershirt, because R.C. told him one day that when he was born there was milk in his breasts. Chacko who is a psychiatrist tells Idiculla that this is common. Idiculla still insists there is something wrong with his chest. So when I find out that Nanjundan will not let anyone touch his chest, and that no one (not even Nina, or Kavita, or Sunni, or that other woman whose name I do not know) has ever seen his chest, I understand that he too has a tale to tell. But he remembers nothing. He has nothing to report. All experience is in symbols for him, and the details don't matter. He collects symbols and structures like a magnet. Everything is deflected to be impressed with the form he sees.

"Kavita," he said.

"Kavita is out," I said.

"Ouuu-nouuu!" Man of few words?

"Would you like to step in?"

Ouuuu-nouuuu. Doglike in his sounds, he rushes into the rain. I go back and lie on my stomach, and I dangle my head out of my bed and from under the bed I watch the rain through the window.

Ganidam is Malayalam for reading the crystal of the future. I have no *ganidam*, then or now. *Ganidam* is not my way.

Kavita made a shocked face. I did not know her very well then. I thought she subscribed to the view that a heart once given away, even when trampled, pines away and is forever constant.

Despite my Nazarene background I myself dream of a time when flinging oneself on the funeral pyre of one's husband was a national ideal. My self-image, no less than his, would have required it. I don't know why, but deep inside I regret the loss of the sati ideal.

Ancient inscriptions tell of the last moments of the woman; she is bathed by women, dressed in saffron robes, distributes alms to the poor, and goes towards the burning pyre *juggling three lemons*.

Now I say, I will burn brightly for a while, burn at both ends, briefly, and be gone.

Hindu art, Hindu drama, even Kathakali was taboo for me. What kind of genetic coding did I receive from my wordless, silent grandmother? Yet Grandmother was Nair; Nairs are a matriarchy. The husband has no function except to help procreate; thereafter, he can be sent about his business at the drop of a pin. All property is supervised by the wife's brother. He is the overseer. Grandmother walked out easily on her Nair stud. She even picked up her one-year-old child.

India grows tea. The British were interested only in cash crops. They grew cotton, tea, indigo. They exported this for profit. They imported staples like rice for profit too. There is nothing as sensational as the economic history of India under the pilfering of the British.

But Mrs Peabody, American, imports tea bags. Her kitchen is full of used ones. Why does she not use Darjeeling tea? Tea bags belonging to different phases of her day can be seen in various spots in her house. She has a friend from middle-west America, pure native brand, as old and zealous as herself, by name and manner, Mrs Fox. When Mrs Fox wants to swear in front of Mrs Peabody she says, "Heck! As my brother-in-law back home used to say, heck!" They both liked to think they were progressives helping the backward, by letting orientals share rooms with whites in white-weary north India. There are places in the south where no man has ever encountered a white face, but here in the north nothing is as déclassé as an Indian woman in western dress.

Mrs Peabody claims that she has introduced detergents into India. Rahel who gets allergies in a cloud of insecticide would laugh the loudest if she heard of what Mrs Peabody considers "revolutionising the underdeveloping countries".

My room at Mrs Peabody's is next to the liquor store. Proximity signifies nothing. I don't drink. Nanjundan does not want to read about exact locations. He knows what lies where. It is no way out to think of him as one abstracted, walking in the clouds to stumble on earth. Ouuuu-nouuuu. He knows the exact location, the streets, the Laundromat—a gift from America, the quadrangle named after Gandhi, the neon pollen at dusk lighting the gaudy fountains in the Plaza; this is neo-India, as magical to some as those pale hands beside the Shalimar were to generations before. Of these things Nanjundan has total recall.

Neon lights are new to India. Khilgesh is new. It is an experiment in a style of life. And no publicist could have thought of better guinea pigs. For who can record better, or jazz up new mores as well as us? A writer is not only a weaver of fantasy, but a blotting pad.

I DON'T KNOW WHY I AM STILL TALKING TO NANJUNDAN. I SHOULD BE PUTTING TEN THOUSAND MILES BETWEEN US. I SHOULD BE IN CALIFORNIA, THE BRAVE NEW WORLD.

What is that I hear? A bus?

3

THE LIMOUSINE FROM SIMLA DROPS ME OUTSIDE THE Porter's Lodge of the writer's farm. To the left of me as far as the eye can go are yellow and ochre and shades of brown downhill. To the right of me the grandiloquence of Victorian Gothic cupolas, porticos, pillars, clock towers, the stamp of the Raj.

There is no one to greet me, meet me, find me a room. There is no telephone in sight. My telegram has been ignored; there is no porter at the lodge.

All my possessions, manuscripts, hundred-odd saris, certificates, credentials, are under me in two boxes. It is hard to believe that Delhi is down there, within a day's journey from this Shangri-La.

It is not just that I came up by road vertically to Khilgesh, through winding streets that dipped and rose, one step back and two forward, but that having got here I could not think easily of descending with an easy mind.

The absence of pedestrians in this mountain hideout makes things extraterrestrial. Everywhere else in India there are masses of moving things, man and beast—jostling.

I walk up the drive and round two buildings. Two adult monkeys and a brood. The male sits over the wide gate; the female breast-feeds.

On seeing me, she says: "Hmmmmmm Hmmmmmmm Hmmmmmm." Startled by that human sound I hurry forward. "Hmmmmmmm, Hmmmmmmm, Hmmmmmmm."

The male gets up on his haunches on the gate and, front paw out, draws back his ample lip and snarling from deep inside, comes at me. Unbidden, I extend my claws, my lips are drawn back exposing thirty teeth, and I snarl back from my patagonian guts. I find myself leaping toward the male monkey.

We made the same sound, the same wild motion of attacking and defending. To my amazement—it was he who turned away. My knees began to knock, and reeling with an ague, I tottered back to where I had hidden my luggage.

Come what may, the worst was over. I gave way to a roar of laughter. Who could have told us apart, the ape in me, the man in him?

The headlights of a car swung past the driveway; the lights made me blink. I was immobile. The car stopped, drove off, turned, and came uphill.

A man in a black sweater got out of it. I did not think of him as Indian. India seemed so far away.

I like the way he laughs at me. Easy laughter. He says life here is lonely. To see another you have to climb a hill. He is the only Indian resident with a car.

His name is Gopal. His home Delhi. He laughs again when he finds out that I have hidden my luggage under a bush.

He finds me a room at Mrs Peabody's. He takes me to his cottage and cooks me a meal of rice and dal. I am not keen on dal, but I like the ride after dinner. He shows me the various cottages, the observation points, the marketplace; and of course, the liquor store right next to Mrs Peabody's.

Then the long smiling silence of the drive round and round Himalayan peaks and as the car whispered past waterfalls, a whisper rose inside me, and came up softly to match his smiling brow and elegant ease at the wheel. Tra-la-la.

Samantha Walker had a theory. "Put the ugliest man and the ugliest women together; isolate them; it is inevitable they will end up desiring each other," she said.

Gopal was by no means ugly; in fact, he was elegant in every little thing he did. To judge from what he said, I was by no means ugly.

"When I see an attractive woman, I cannot touch her."

I said, something shooting into my heart, "You don't have to touch," and thought, a glance, is sometimes as unbearable as touch. I looked at his lips.

At the door of his little cottage, Gopal said, "I have been a celibate for years. My work keeps me isolated. A writer's life is lonely, as you must know. I also work on the farm. Everything we make goes into common funds, but a lot of the fellows here have either savings or outside help. Money does not seem to matter here, except for those who drink. I work on the farm till I am about to drop; then I sit here on the porch, with a branch of the tree over my head, and brood."

"Why? You don't strike me as naturally that way."

"For five years I lived with a girl. Zebunnissa, a Muslim girl. When the time came for us to marry, I told her I was a Brahmin and could not. She rushed into a marriage with an orthodox Muslim who keeps her in purdah. She has never been seen anywhere since. I know she is miserable, and I can never return to Delhi."

Our most characteristic act freezes us. We are forever reliving our most characteristic moment. Everything is a replication of that *idee fixe*, even our writing which is one more grimace expressing that moment.

"Why, Gopal, why?"

I stroke his hand. My fingers play on his palm, I press the tips of his fingers. He pulls me towards him, sinks his teeth into my neck, and leaves a bloody bite mark on the left side of my neck. Then he leaps up and runs into his little kitchen, and pours himself a drink of water from the surai.

Love is for me the most unbearable of emotions.

Love makes me feel I will explode. The fear is very strong. For years I have let life flow by me. I have not permitted touch. Touch is therapy, touch is salvation; where touch is life is; it is the least common factor in life; it is the last of the senses.

I see everything now; a glance, a shade of thought, nuances all interior—they emerge and dazzle. Nuances all interior prompt the thought that eyes are x-ray, and the heart cobalt, and atoms of all beings float around. Conscious things attract all conscious things.

4

KAVITA COMES TO BORROW COLD CREAM. SHE IS WEARING Bermudas. No woman looks glamorous in shorts that come down but expose the knees. Glamour in shorts requires the contrast of thigh and calf, the dimples of knees smiling in between.

"The mini-sari will never work, not unless it stops way above the knees," says Miriam, the dark-haired Lebanese woman Kavita has acquired. Miriam is the freest person in Khilgesh; she makes no bones about it. Kavita spends all her time with Miriam.

Kavita started with her feet and worked her way up.

Both women were concentrating on Kavita's legs. I thought she wanted cold cream for her face. Now watching her fingers travelling back and forth from her legs to the jar, I don't want the jar anymore.

"You can keep the whole jar," I told her.

"I just want to put a little more on my legs; they are so dry," she said, looking at them admiringly as she bent over, her hair trailing on the floor.

"I have been taking out all the snarls out of her hair. Do you have something that will go through knotted hair?"

"Try a fork," I said, meaning a pitchfork.

"Mira, what are you doing this evening?" She usually put Foo Yang through a third-degree trying to find out my movements. Foo Yang moves silently, except when cooking. She sees more than she tells Kavita. I have no problems with Foo Yang.

"Gopal has asked me for a movie tonight. I saw it in Delhi and in Bombay, but I think I will see it a third time," I said.

Kavita started demonstrating how she practices in front of the mirror on how to look seductive. It looked to me like maxillary convulsions, as if someone was torturing her at the other end. I did not think it a waste of her time.

I am dressed and ready. I wait at the window. But Gopal does not turn up. At two a.m. I see him opening the door of the car; Kavita is wearing a dazzling blue Kanchipuram sari, I see in the light of the gatepost that she has long ear things dangling—they flash at me. I see them everywhere together after that. Inseparable. I avoid Gopal.

One day, I saw Nanjundan flirting with Kavita.

After bed, I said to him, sitting up naked in his room, "Nanjundan, why do you flirt with Kavita? I saw you in the coffee shop at night yesterday. If you want her that bad, why don't you have her?"

"I have had her."

I weep inconsolably. He lets me cry. He seems to enjoy it.

"Why didn't you tell me?"

"How could I? I have my loyalties to her; I could not just blurt it out. I told you now that you have asked me. She talks of you a lot. But you don't. I respect you for that."

I have no answer to that.

Alfred, who is fascinated by all things Indian, particularly folklore and myth, returns from the library. As soon as he comes in Nanjundan says as usual, "Why don't you run along now, Mira?"

"As a matter of fact I was going to reach Mira home," said the man from Ann Arbor.

The night air is cool, and we walk to Mrs Peabody's across two lawns and a short rise.

At the door, Alfred shoots a strange glance at me. I am baffled.

Whenever I am with Nanjundan, Alfred sees me home. I cannot believe he is an American. He is just like an Indian. Next time at dinner with them, I say to Alfred, "Alfred, you are just like an Indian."

"And you are just like the girl next door, in Ann Arbor, Michigan. I feel I have known you all my life. Something familiar."

"Yes," said Nanjundan, "a familiar kind of smell!"

Alfred continues to see me home. One day, Nanjundan surprised us by offering to walk me back. In front of Mrs Peabody's cottage, he pulls me down on the ground, unbuttons his fly and sticks his organ into my mouth. Nothing has prepared me for it; none of the romances I read. Egg whites spilled into my mouth, a hair that will not be dislodged lodges permanently in my throat; I go upstairs and retch till my guts are in my throat.

5

I AM IN THE WOODS OUTSIDE THE FARM. I LEAN AGAINST a tree. Whenever I am alone I spin my kaleidoscope backward into time and forward into space. I rehearse endlessly, past, present, and future.

Peter Bradstreet joins me. I am not aware of his presence at first. When I notice him, I cannot manage a smile, so deep am I with images of Nanjundan.

He grabs his sandwiches. He has the American habit of carrying around stale bread and eating it for lunch.

"Will it bother you if I eat this?"

"Oh no!" I said, and immediately my mouth starts flooding. Trying to swallow I begin coughing.

"What's your problem?"

"What do you mean—what's my problem?"

"You are defensive."

"I don't know what that means."

Peter does not drink or smoke. He avoids Coke, coffee, tea; all noxious according to him. I puzzle over this.

"That sounds defensive, too," he said.

"The hell it does!" I said.

"Don't swear, foul language fouls up the mind."

"Americans love four-letter words."

"And you?"

"I don't like fuck or shit, but bullshit turns me on."

"What's your problem?"

"I have been sleeping with a friend of mine for the last so many months and he cannot enter me."

"Has he tried digital manipulation?" He said it casually.

"What's that?"

"Used his fingers."

I am shocked. Speechless.

"Why? Can't you give it to yourself? Have you never given it to yourself?"

"No. I am not being defensive. I can't explain. I have yet to become a woman."

"That you are! That you are!"

"What I mean is that I grew up with nuns."

"There you go again. Don't blame the nuns. Why don't you see a doctor? Here, I will write down for you the name of my wife's gynaecologist; go see him. He is a remarkable man."

Dr Frisk was remarkable, but I did not see him for another year. Nanjundan, when told of the doctor, said, "You can do that for your own purposes."

Peter walks away abruptly. Always quick to learn, the lesson emerges as, ALL MANIPULATIONS ARE ESSENTIALLY DIGITAL.

Gopal begs me to go see him. I go reluctantly.

"What is this strange relationship between you and Kavita?" he shouts.

"Don't shout; it is so unlike you. There is no strange relationship. I just want to avoid having anything to do with her. I want her to get off my trail. I am hiding from her."

"She is interested in me only when she thinks you are interested in me. Last week, she came to my room because she was in your room when I called you to borrow some money from you."

I was silent, and he continued, "Well, she came here and offered herself to me for the first time."

"Well, well, well. Why for the first time?"

"It's a long story. I don't know how I have fallen so low!"

"Why didn't you take me for the Satyajit Ray movie? I was dressed and waiting."

"Kavita came to my workshop and said that you wanted me to take her instead, since you have seen the movie."

"Would I do that?"

"Maybe I needed to believe what she said."

"A flattering thought! I waited for you all night."

He ignored that and continued, "Kavita asked me to support her. I agreed to do that. She has run through my savings. Later she said we could get married. Then she said we could get married, but we won't have any sex. She works me up. She acts chaste one day, and the next day she is seducing some other man. She drops broad hints. You won't believe it, she has reduced me to a footpath watcher outside her window, while she seduces others with her window lit. That is why she has moved out of Mrs Peabody's. How have I fallen so low!"

"Gopal, I am going to tell you a secret; now don't go and blurt it out to Kavita. I am in love with Nanjundan. I might even marry him. If I am not seen in public with him, it is because I don't want Kavita to see us together. Nanjundan does not want to be seen in public with me, because of Nina. It works out fine. When I am with Nanjundan, Alfred who shares a cottage with Nanjundan—as you know—sees me home. I go out socially with the Arab, Ismail. He is very companionable."

"Kavita can't make up her mind whether it is me you want, or Alfred, or Ismail. You have been quite clever."

"No, I have no skills to match her skills. If I play her game, I will come out second best. She has been telling everyone she is younger than me. I dare not tell anyone that she is several years my senior. She is even older than Nanjundan. I told her that I once fled from an Australian because he turned anthropologist on me. Now she has written a first person narrative and shown it to Aiyer. She parodies me till I sound like a parody of her."

"Why is she unmarried, Mira?"

"I can't tell you. I know too much about her. It's bad for me to talk about her. It's none of my business."

"You don't hate me, do you, Mira?"

"I don't hate easily, or love easily, Gopal."

"Can I ask you something?" says Gopal, and I smile.

"That mysterious smile. How can I ask, when you smile like that?"

"All right, I will think of the sad death of King George the Sixth."

"This is meant well. Are you happy with Nanjundan?"

"That is none of your business."

"I have been here some years now. I know everyone here. They say he gets into difficulties with every woman he meets."

"What's your interest in Nanjundan? I did not think you gossiped like an old woman."

"Mira, I have known for some time that you have been seeing him."

"You make me panic; you won't blurt it out in your sleep to Kavita, will you?" I said, reclining on his divan.

"I told you we don't sleep together."

"My sympathies!"

"Don't be nasty, Mira. I think I will drive you home."

"Please don't bother," I said, curling up. Then I jumped up, saying, "Well, why not? There is always the chance that Kavita will see us together. That will keep her off the scent of Nanjundan!"

"Don't let her distort you, Mira. I am no longer a man. I don't know what I am. I am beginning to sympathise with murderers these days. I know what it is like to want to kill someone."

"She is a very gifted woman. She knows how to turn heroes into hogs." Needless to say, we exchanged not a word or glance on the way home.

Peter comes into my mind sometimes. He speaks like a lone prophet occasionally, a side of him that fills me with doublethink. He has given his whole life to the theatre.

Phullora, my dead illiterate maid, gave hers to the "cinema". Everything was a rehearsal for the camera eye.

In Kuttapuzha I grew like a young jack tree.

How far have I travelled? How many miles is it from Kuttapuzha to Khilgesh? How many stops from land's end to the roof of the world?

For some time now I have been reading a poem written in a madhouse over two centuries ago. In those days, people paid to watch the day's compulsive acts in asylums.

I feel now the eyes of watchers watching the watchers watching Khilgesh. The *Jubilate Agno* by Christopher Smart is a fine model for the Indians at Khilgesh. Smart, unlike Peter, is essentially a woman. Most gifted men are part female. Does this mean Peter is not gifted? Smart is also a manic depressive.

When happy, he cries:

For innumerable ciphers will amount to something.

For infinite upon infinite they make a chain.

He uses metaphors and parables like an Indian woman making a garland.

He uses large categories like "light" and "dark"—as if he was massing armies on opposite sides for a mock battle.

For Smart, the glory of creation is not clouded by the dust of the crucifixion. This is an old thought of mine and I find it in him.

Are the fir trees of Lebanon trees? Or are they the kings and princesses of the gentiles? The exterior is distant from the interior, but he who is mad insinuates secretly. I should know, for I am as mad as Kit Smart.

What is Jerusalem to you? What is Kuttapuzha to me?

My spirit whirls up over the fir trees of Lebanon. And I see a chain about Orpheus, about the psalmist David, about the Harp.

Half the lines begin with the word Let. The imperative, the masculine, the He. Let there be Light.

The other half being with the word For. The response of the ongoing, of the woman. For I am a frog in the brambles and the Lord has put his whole armour upon me. "Let" says the versicle. "For" says the response. Male and female made he them.

The male is not merely a question of voice, beard, hat on the head—though Christopher Smart is obsessed with these. So am I. So am I.

Then there is the betwixt and the between, the oil and water of discord. The Judeo-Christian and cabalistic marriage of heaven and hell. Images of dark and images of light.

Between and betwixt is the commonly got and highly personal horn. Now a megaphone in the sky, now a sexual organ, and finally the horn of plenty and the horn of honey and milk.

I feel exhausted. My head burst with bubbles. My stomach feels full of termites. My lips hurt from too much coffee. I long for a hand to soothe my hair, a voice to lull me to sleep. We are all infants in our thirst. I too desire to be suckled. When I read or think, I need most someone to hold my breasts.

Born with a mother, always looking for a father, I worship all strong old men. A centre against which I rage, and for which I hurtle like a magnet. Peter is older than anyone else writing on the Farm.

Ismail Ibrahim speaks in Arabic sometimes. He looks like a zombie. Behind that lean look lies a heart as passionate as that of Habib the cook, in Aden. I am at ease with him. We enjoy movies. He speaks French occasionally to me. Surprisingly, he is civilised. One day after lunch things get out of hand.

"*Allons, allez, chez mois,*" he says.

"*Non, monseuer! Pardonne.*"

"Why, what's the matter with you, Mira?"

"Why, what's the matter with me?"

"A man looks into your eyes and he drowns. It is a bottomless pool."

"Ismail, I am not free. I thought you knew, respected it."

"Yes, it must be that. But he must be a phantom, whoever he is."

"I am thinking of getting married to Nanjundan."

"You can't be serious!"

"Why, what's the objection?"

"Why would a girl like you want to get married? Too many women get married and return looking like charwomen. Marriage is obsolete."

"I agree. I have no objection to living in sin. But it has to be with a single person. I am by nature monogamous."

"My background is very different."

"Yes, I know the Nizam of Hyderabad has as many wives as there are days in the year. What did the women do, till he got around to them?"

"I get the impression that Indian women are virtuous," he smiles.

"If Indian women are virtuous, why do people insist that widows shave off their hair, and eat a prison fare without lentils or anything nutritious?"

"Do you want to see the Punjabi opera, *Heer Ranjha*?" said Ismail. "It starts in two hours. We can spend the afternoon in the woods."

"I will meet you at the opera, I'll go back to Mrs. Peabody's."

"I will come and fetch, an hour and a half from now." He seemed to be in a good mood.

At the opera, *Heer Ranjha*, I see Nanjundan walking ten paces behind Nina. But he sits next to her, his arms crossed. Alfred is there too.

After the opera, Alfred comes with us to Ismail's for beer. Nanjundan leaves the opera ten paces ahead of Nina.

The graffiti on Ismail's wall never fails to fascinate me. It is done in invisible ink, visible only with a particular kind of light.

At the opera, I had seen Clare from Brooklyn. She has dark hair, and dark skin. Could pass for a Punjabi girl. She walks differently from Indian girls. She has been very gloomy off late, she has stopped seeing Ignazio, a firebrand Spanish writer. He wanted her, a Jew, to become a Catholic. I talked to her a lot about Alfred, and talked to Alfred about her. Typically, her spirits rose—every time I spoke of the kindest man I had ever met. She said, she would like to meet him. I told her that she could come with me the next time I dined with Nanjundan.

I said to Alfred, "Did you see Clare during the interval? I want you to meet her. Can she come for dinner?"

Alfred's face turned red. He did not look up, but lowering his head, he said, "I don't need a go-between. Tell me something, how long does it take for a nice girl to come?" With that he threw a glance at the coffee table and left.

"Want some tissue, want a handkerchief?" said Ismail, seeing my tears.

"No, I want to go home. I feel I am no longer where I am, but in some foreign country." I cry all night.

6

MRS. PEABODY TOOK ME TO CHURCH, IN SIMLA. SHE introduced me around as a rich merchant's daughter from the south. A passing tourist with a preposterous face asked me facetiously if the bindi on my forehead was a trickle of blood. Nanjundan would call such a remark a stroke, but the bindi is a sore point with me. I wear it as a mark of self-respect. It is my declaration of independence from Nestorian Kerala, where it is a sign of devil worship. The tourist is well aware that Indian Christians don't usually wear bindis. I said to him, "No, I don't trickle there, do you?"

Mrs. Peabody is offended. Rich merchant's daughter! What do you expect, milady?

All progressives have shibboleths. Like Mrs Smith in Bombay, Mrs Peabody says, "All our bodily functions are the same!"

Dear Mrs Peabody, ask the physical anthropologists, they will tell you something different.

Gopal begs me to visit him again. He is in trouble.

"I don't feel like coming to see you," I said firmly.

"I can't come there; your landlady hates men."

"I can't come to your office; offices distort me."

"We can't be seen in public!" said Gopal. "You will have to come to the Mall. I will meet you there."

"What if Kavita sees us?" I said, hoping he would let things be.

"There is a small chance she will care now," he said. That decided me; I ran all the way to the Mall. If she has broken with Gopal, she would be on a rampage again. I did not want her to know about me and Nanjundan. When I got there, I ordered a coke. Gopal came in and said, "Did you tell Ismail that you were going to marry Nanjundan?" he barked.

"Yes," I said sheepishly.

"Well, he told her." His glance accused me.

"How could he?"

"Why wouldn't he?"

"Oh God!"

"She came to see me today and announced brutally, 'It's not you Mira is after, but Nanjundan. But Mira does not know that Nanjundan writes me love letters. You see, I jilted him. But I can always have him back!'"

"What did you say to that?"

"I have learnt to show no emotion. I try to control myself. She likes to see me jump like a monkey on hot bricks."

"That takes care of one person. Good work Kavita, old girl!"

"She left me, and then rushed back with her laundry. Like a fool I rose to the bait. I went to do her laundry, as she often leaves her laundry with me. Don't laugh at me.

I don't know how I have fallen so low. I did her laundry; in it was this chiffon sari. A gift of love from Nanjundan. What sort of man is this Nanjundan whom you say you are marrying—if he gives another woman a sari as a 'gift of love'?"

Strange things happen. A machine, a gift of love from America, changes life around Khilgesh. In the old days, women fought at the village well. But the character of the machine has changed the nature of the fight. Occasionally the electricity fails, but the well too dried up during drought. Gopal left me sitting with my Coke; he could not stand the fact that I was amused at his predicament. He offered compensation up to a thousand rupees, money he could now ill afford. But she says, "It can never be replaced; it is a gift of love."

Things that happen to Nanjundan don't really happen to him. He is absent. He is not there. He goes through the motions of being used. Being rejected. Being everybody's doormat. Nanjundan is a paradox. He does not make sense to me. I don't claim to understand him. He draws with a brush dipped in acid. In direct contrast to his satirical writings, in his own life he is open-minded. He refuses to judge. I leave that to others, he says.

Nanjundan and I watched a street murder in the bazaar, and all that Nanjundan could say was: "What strange green eyes the dead woman has!"

He is a Hindu. A Brahmin. Recently, I throw all his clothes out. Even his shoes and ties. Out of the house. His things just lay there in our front garden till everything began to rot. In the end, I had to pick them up and discard them.

It snows. My first snow. It lifts me up to the top of the mountain. So flaky, it falls endlessly. Melts in my hands, on my tongue held out for more. Prints my footprints along the winding path. There where no other has stepped before me. They turn the drab exteriors of cottages into picturebook houses of sugar candy; candied twigs on bare branches bring back pictures of Carrot's childhood; they float back from never-never land. White, the poetry of whiteness. Soft. Sound is different. The occasional car that comes by, no longer whispers. Everything is still. My voice is loud. I begin to whisper. Music. I hear it everywhere. I hear sleigh bells in my mind. I leap on skis down mountain slopes in my mind. I lie on snow. I lick it off rocks. I rub my face in it. I make snowballs for my windowsill. I feel energy. I run up and down the hill. It's snowing. It's snowing. I whisper to strangers who smile.

Ismail Ibrahim turns up. He gives me an expensive gift. I am reminded of Samantha Walker. The scarfs of Yugoslavia, the perfumes of France.... I go upstairs and I weep, for her, for me, for everyone. I weep till my eyes have cataracts in them. He waits outside. He suggests we go somewhere. Why not to Nanjundan? Why not? Nanjundan is not alone. Alfred is there. I go into the kitchen for coffee. Alfred says between locked jaws, his American sense of what's proper, affronted by me for the first time: "You are the only girl I know who takes one date out to meet another."

I see things. I see the chimney against the light of the sky. I see the green of windows against the oblongs of housefronts and the lime-wash of walls. I see light bouncing back and forth.

There is this haze in front of me. Through it, all things are distant but luminescent. I see Alfred, I see Ismail, I see Nanjundan. I sit blockstill. Everything is restored to harmony. I cannot move. I see Nanjundan's eyes; they are incandescent. They are the most wondrous things I have ever seen; they glow outwards, from inside outwards with embers of feeling.

Seeing me turn to mutton, Nanjundan makes me drink alcohol. He takes away my coffee. One, two, three times, he serves me scotch. After a few more, my vision clears. I see with clarity the lines of Nanjundan's face. The haze disappears with alcohol.

7

NANJUNDAN HAS GIVEN UP HIS ROOM WITH ALFRED AND is living with Gopal.

"No!" I am shocked. I no longer see him where he lives; we meet at odd times in the woods.

"What's wrong with living with Gopal?" he said.

"Will you never learn a lesson?"

He is silent, smiling to himself.

"That woman has been working on Gopal. That is why you are where you are. Remember that sari you bought for her?"

"I bought no sari for her."

"Yes, you did, Nanjundan. I had a grey chiffon sari. She wanted to know where I got it. I wouldn't tell her. To tease me you went with her to Simla. You did! You said you paid for it because she talked so loud in the shop about not having money. Well, she is twisting Gopal's arm by saying it is a gift of love from you."

"What has that to do with him?"

"It has plenty to do with him. She made him launder her clothes at the American washing machine. Since he is a novice at laundering saris, it came out mangled. He offered her thousands of rupees for it, but she is like one demented; she says it can never be replaced; it is a gift of love."

"That is something between them. How do you know all this?"

"Gopal told me," I said, spitefully.

"I don't believe half of what he tells you. What's his game? She does not strike me that way."

"How does she strike you?"

"She is talented and lovely; she is unhappy and we should not add to her unhappiness."

"She might seem lovely to you, but she gives me the creeps."

"You are prejudiced. Let's not discuss it any more."

"Nanjundan, you and I don't see anything eye to eye—do we? I don't see why you want me to tag along."

"Mira, you and I read the same books. We laugh at the same jokes. The moment I saw you, I saw diapers drying in the sun. I am a Brahmin and this is my last life. We should get married. Then everything will take care of itself. I would like to change you a bit, change the colour schemes of your saris for example."

"What about the haggard girl we met at the store, whose name I do not know, and who asked after your friend Jaya? Why don't you tell me her name, so that I don't have to refer to her as the girl in the store who asked after your friend?"

"She belongs to the past. Her name is not important. If I tell you her name, you will turn it into a mantra. I don't want to hear her name. I am not interested in her anymore. I knew she was waiting for me at the store. She told me so. I took you with me. That took care of her. Having seen you, she knows that she won't find it easy now, making a comeback!"

"What about Nina, what if she wants you back, like this girl does?"

"We will cross that bridge when we come to it."

"What about Kavita?"

"She does not mean a thing to me."

"Then why are you staying at Gopal's?"

"Because she offered to put me up there. Nina is staying there too."

"O God! What is Kavita? Is she a procuress?"

"I have affections for them. She said to me casually, 'There is a couch in the living room; you can sleep there, but the springs creak.'"

"Did they creak?"

"Cut it out, Mira; you don't expect me to break off every relationship because of you."

"And what is Nina doing meantime?"

"She is knitting booties for Miriam's baby."

"Aha! I get the picture. What shall I do that will wring Nanjundan's heart? Something homely, something feminine. Knitting booties, indeed! What next?"

"She has cut her hair; when we were together I made her promise that she would grow her hair, and when I looked at her shorn head, she winced."

"Keep the romance to yourself, Nanjundan."

"There is no romance; everyone knows she is living openly with Aiyer; she has just moved in with Gopal because Aiyer's wife has come up from the south where she lives in Pondicherry at the Ashram.

"Oh God! Will this never end?"

"Will you marry me, Mira? If I act strangely, remember, I am only half a man. If you walk out on me now, no one will ever see me again."

There is something in a girl that makes her accept a man who has wounded her, the moment he offers matrimony. Is this social or biological? The most important questions in life have no real answers. Yet, once we ask such a question, everything looks different.

8

TEN DAYS BEFORE THE WEDDING, NANJUNDAN MOVED into the cottage we now live in. He borrowed two extra stoves and started me on cooking for all and sundry. No sooner would I finish one meal, he would bring in more people. He insisted that I make dosa and idli and payasam and all the time-consuming south Indian dishes. The lentils had to be soaked overnight, ground on a stone (Rahel has two electric blenders!) and cooked the next morning. There would be breakfast parties, lunch parties, tea parties, and dinner parties. People came to eat; there was hardly any conversation. The idea of a cocktail party is a foreign idea. Each guest had a distinct style of eating. Just as there is a linguistic map of India, one could easily chart another equally confusing map of culinary and gustatory customs. Standing over six burners, my head swam; my feet ached. The sauna and steam of cooking gave me a baker's complexion. I forget I had lived any other way. It looked natural to be doing what I did. In fact, I had lost the ability to step out of the cottage or cross the street by myself.

We went down to Simla to get married. On the way in the train going downhill, Nanjundan said, "That girl at the station...."

"Which girl?"

"The one I was talking to. She is to me what Gopal was to you. I was engaged to her once. But she left for Bombay. She is a hostess at the Taj Mahal."

"What! How many times have you been engaged, Nanjundan?" Ignoring my question, he said, "She went away to Bombay. Whenever I went to Bombay, she had breakfast, lunch, and dinner engagements and she saw me in between. The boot was on the other foot this time; when she came to Khilgesh, we were so busy! She has a trunk filled with cards and tags she has collected from the gifts she received from admirers."

"She wants to retire with her trophies now?"

"Well, she wants me back now. She was out of her depths when I first met her. Now that she has seen the world, she says such things don't count between a man and a woman."

"Fill me in, Nanjundan. What *does* count between a man and a woman?"

"I think she has had a taste of adventure and now wants a sober life with me."

"And you?"

"How would you like it if you walked out on me today, and returned to me years later begging me to take you in and found me indifferent?"

All things are equidistant, he had said. He stood in the centre, and this nameless girl and I, along with God knows how many others, stood at the circumference. His question hung like a low cloud, and I said steeling myself, "That is a very big if. I never return to my vomit like a sick dog. This girl has rings under the eyes. She looks a wreck. Of course I have read that some men just cannot resist consumptives and whores. She is not even bright. Definitely dim. She doesn't even have a decent pair of breasts."

"She has a fine pair of breasts."

"How would you know? She stood you up, remember!"

"She came here to Gopal's, undressed, we got into the creaky couch. I had a tremendous erection, and she said, 'O dear, you are going to hurt the girls.' You never say such things to me. But Gopal, Nina and Kavita, returned...."

"How could you! This is the end. It's all over between us."

"What's over?"

"Everything."

"If you leave me now, I will kill myself." He leaped up. His veins looked engorged. The train went into a tunnel. The lights came on. His muscles felt like steel; I held on to him; he was making for the door. The train made a horrible din, creaking, clattering, shuddering. I felt the moisture from the tunnel; there were waterfalls in the tunnel. The train lurched suddenly, and as I was heaving with all my might, we fell sideways.

When I came to, Nanjundan's face was anxious. He smiled as if nothing had happened.

At the Cathedral, on the way to the ceremony, in the presence of a gathering of strangers and acquaintances Nanjundan said, "Mira, why don't we call the whole thing off?"

After the ceremony, conducted by a visiting minister of unknown denomination, we came out into the sunlight.

Jaya and Thampi, Nanjundan's neighbours from high-school days were outside. They had not come into the church. When we reached the end of the lane leading to the Victorian Cathedral, Nanjundan's cousin-in-law Rao, who lives at the Institute for Advanced Study, turned up.

"Why are you wearing white?" said Jaya.

"Until recently my people wore only white. Now they wear white for all rituals."

"Among Hindus, only widows wear white. It is very inauspicious; so even widows try not to wear white. Why aren't you wearing any jewellery?"

"My people don't wear jewellery."

"Why didn't you buy some costume jewellery here in Simla?"

"Would I wear baubles, if I don't wear diamonds?"

I thought the girl had bad manners. She had gold on her mind. Nanjundan was the third of six sons, and though traditionally he could have deflowered me with impunity, his marriage would never have been recognised. I myself had trouble informing H.C. about Nanjundan. There was no language in which to communicate it. No woman of breeding would choose a mate on her own, and that too one so alien. I wasted whole reams trying to write a letter, but in the end gave it up. I had to make a clean break. There was no way in which I could tell H.C. that I was marrying one Mr. Nanjundan, biologist by training, satirist by choice; born in Nagercoil in 1931 of Namboodiri parents and living in the north where he could converse with people only in embarrassed English, going through the motions of being everyone when secretly he was more Namboodiri than most Namboodiris.... No, there was no way I could do that. Each sentence would have infuriated H.C. I saw no pleasure in bear-baiting.

Nanjundan's schoolfellow Thampi looked like he had just taken a purgative. A purge once a month was quite the fashion in the south. Yet, the first thing he said to me was, "I am hungry. We did not eat anything since we left Egmore station."

"We can eat at the West End Hotel," I said.

"We don't eat out," said the Brahmins in a chorus. I have seen them eat out on several occasions since. Perhaps their backs were up! Was it not the responsibility of the bride's family to feed the groom's family? Or, maybe they had to be a party to initiating me in the ways of Brahminhood, alias *pattardom*, alias beggardom, alias boordom.

Nanjundan suggested that I go with him to a flat he could borrow from one of the scholars residing at the Institute for Advanced Study. Rao did not have a flat—only a room, but he knew of a place we could use for the day.

Nanjundan then made me change my white sari, which was beginning to make him feel *rigor mortis*, he said. I put on the loudest sari in my possession. I went down the many steps and alleys to the bazaar; there I bought turmeric, chilli, salt, coriander, onion, carrots, beans, cucumber, butter, and rice; I had forgotten dal, so I went back and got some. The butter melted on the way back. I began to smell like a Brahmin.

Nanjundan met me at the top of the hill. He said that his cousin-in-law Rao did not eat onions, that Jaya and Thampi did not eat garlic.

"This is not me," I told myself. "It is true my parents were strange, but my mother meant to invite five hundred people to the Taj and among them there would have been at least some two-fifty who had been at one time or another companions-in-crime in the many schools I attended!"

Nanjundan's friend Thampi was a touchstone for Nanjundan. If Thampi had no objection, all would have been well. But Thampi said in an aside, loud enough for me to hear, "If you had to come this far, why marry a girl from your own state, and that too outside the caste?"

Nanjundan grinned and grimaced. I studied Thampi—he was tall and dark and looked like the spitting image of a priest in the Padmanabhan temple in Trivandrum. Even from him I could not gather anything about Nanjundan's background. Nanjundan and Thampi exchanged glances when Thampi said that Nanjundan's father was a freedom fighter who died in jail. But Nanjundan said his father was a mountaineer, and that was why Nanjundan had come to Khilgesh.

He said, "It takes a generation for dreams to come true—a father's dreams become the son's or grandson's reality."

Nanjundan said that his father was so strong, the children lived in terror of him. Mother was everything. She lived in the kitchen. Father ate alone, first. Then the children were fed. Finally the mother ate by herself.

Jaya watched me cook. She was laughing about her own wedding: even an abridged version of the ceremony ran into several days. All kinds of Vedic items like leaves and coconuts figured in it.

To make matters worse, the Americans on the Farm sent us a present of plastic everlasting flowers. The countryside is full of flowers, and the Americans sent us plastic flowers. More than cooking, more than the strangeness of strangers, the sight of those monstrous flowers finished the day for me. After that, I went steadily downhill.

When everybody left, Nanjundan stripped with speed. He tore the peacock blue off me. He put on the ceiling light. He was like one possessed. He tore my organs. He stuffed his finger up my urethra. His hair flew in every direction. He seemed to say with every thrust of his nails, "See, I have made an honest woman of you! My gods of reason and loyalty, loyalty to caste, mother, and religion—all set aside for you. Thirty years of bachelordom all down for nothing. And I am trapped by you."

He said to me, "You are ugly, you have no charm."

He watched us in the mirror. I felt like something on display.

Answer me something, you out there! Every pig has it; why have I been cheated out of anything instinctual? What's my crime?

Months of cooking round the clock and there's mutiny. I was making chapatis when I suddenly threw down the rolling pin and said, "I won't stand for this any more."

"Why, what's the matter, what next?" said Nanjundan in a reasonable voice.

"What's the matter! I won't cook for your women friends any more. That woman Sunni—well, she can go find herself a cook."

"She is a vegetarian and a Brahmin; she will starve."

"Then let her starve. There are many vegetarian and Brahmins in Khilgesh; they don't starve."

"You are mean and suspicious."

"I won't take this any more, I am leaving."

"Do you want me to slit my throat?"

At the door he put one hand through the glass pane, and then the other hand; his flesh exposed, he lay there in a pool of blood.

We rushed him to a hospital.

There he shouted, "I will sue you if I die!" I started laughing.

After they had stitched him up, Nanjundan smiled and said, "She is not important to me. Let Sunni go eat garlic; I don't really care. She is only an old spinster. She used to be any ideal. I had fantasies about her. But now I know it's you I want, Mira!" I had no response to that. I had become hard of hearing. So he shouted, "My brilliant fool!"

Are there women who can turn themselves on and off like a water tap? If so, I'd like to meet them: I need that trick myself.

9

THE INDIAN COFFEE HOUSE AT MADRAS. THE MAIN floor is divided into two sections by an arched doorway. They frowned when I lit a cigarette. Over the arched partition is a board with red on white. It says: "SILENCE REQUESTED". Noisy temples and silent coffee houses in Madras.

I scratched my head with maniacal fury till the scalp is sore. I notice it is not an allergy but lice. I find one in my nail. Travelling three nights by third class in a train, you acquire an army of lice. (I am glad I left Baby with Nanjundan and an ayah.) I comb out the lice on to a white sheet. Thumb over thumb, I kill the lice. I cannot quite understand the peculiar kind of glee and disgust with which I squash each louse.

Dinner at the Gaylord restaurant in Madras recalls old Mrs Walker: "What the good Lord gives, the gay lord takes away." The eloquence of the restaurant is a false rhetoric. Nothing goes well in Madras as well as a Brahmin dosa-and-coffee restaurant. Dosas are the only combustibles to be filmed in the south. Large as a table, served in stainless steel "ever-silver" thalis, they are golden and crisp, often rolled with masala. But the Gaylord serves nothing southern. Northern, western, far eastern, you name it; but none of this south of Karnatak nonsense will be dished up. The Gaylord has therefore an air of intrigue about it.

A fat, dark man sits with an air of earnestness next to an indifferent Caucasian woman. It is enough to breathe her breath. He studies the sauce bottles, particularly the chilli sauce. He reads it like he would the label of vintage wines, had there been no prohibition in Madras. Slowly, like an elegant butler stooping deferentially, he hands it to the Causasian woman in the churidar-pajamas sitting next to him, with silent approval.

The band starts blaring. The singer has a long-legged look; she is toothy. Remembering Nanjundan's enthusiasm for Nina's fangs, I wondered where he was.

I have to go see Nanjundan's mother. She has requested me to see her. This I call progress. At least I exist. I am recognised. They know I exist. They have asked for me.

There is a blare of wind instruments. In the spotlight appears "Luscious Loraine in the strip!" In Madras, the tight virginal city, "Luscious Loraine" doing the pelvic dance, however eloquent the pelvis, is met with sneers and leers, and general squirming at every table. Rahel's words come back to me—"Anything misplaced is dirt!"

I start out in search of Nanjundan's mother. She is visiting Madras. Her home is in Nagercoil. She is visiting her nephew who lives in the Brahmin *agraharam* to the north of the city, the last refuge of the pure Brahmin.

I ask women with velvet for skin and eyes limpid with light, the way to the house of K.R.C. Aiyar. On the way, I pass a shirtless Brahmin with a resplendent *namam* on his brow. The designs on his forehead and chest are made with sandalwood and kumkum, his *kudumbi* a gleaming, loose knot; his earrings and his upright carriage arrest my attention; he looks like a stage Brahmin. He is seventy years old. I look at him with interest. To my horror he stops, and wiggling his brows, his eyes merry, he gives me the gladdest of glad eyes. I am horrified. Two notions are in the dust: one, the saintliness of old age, and two, the celibacy of a pujari or priest. Had not H.C. become a complete human being with approaching old age? Had not Grandfather been the nearest thing to God?

In Dostoevsky, there is a man who but dreamt of a child trying to seduce him, and he, the dreamer, on waking put a bullet through his own head because he did not want to live in a world where a child would try and seduce a grown man. Bruno Bettelheim, faced with an actual child trying to seduce him, sent for the child's mother, and his investigations proved that the mother had been fornicating in front of the child who stood in the crib watching, while the mother earned her living thus. What was unthinkable for the nineteenth century man, the twentieth century man could not only study, but could also attempt to cure!

I found the house. It was a whole block of houses, six units in a block, with a common lavatory and bathroom. The front of each unit has an open drain. My spine tingled.

On one side of the main room, the wall was decorated with calendars. A calendar gallery. Mrs Peabody collected string and old hosiery, but she hid it in her basement smelling of rotting potatoes. Here, they collected calendars of every year. They even had one for the next year. With one exception. There was, high on the wall, out of harm's way, a row of umbrellas and a picture of President Kennedy.

A Brahmin among Brahmins?

Across the room was a string on which were thrown garments of every description. I thought I saw a G-string. In the backroom, glimpsed through the open doorway, were polished silver plates, copper and brass vessels. They reflected a rich metallic glow as did the complexions of the women.

Three men sat on the verandah, in dhotis, and spoke faultless English to one another. They ignored me altogether.

I stood at the doorstep. Then I saw her. She needed dental care. Her tooth wiggled and smiled. There was an extra thumb on her right hand. She had stiff joints from old age. She still cooked and served.

As I stared at her slight form, something extraordinary happened. Her face is the face of one who has never complained, who would never complain. She owns nothing, would own nothing. She touches everything, but nothing would touch her. Her feet are bare.

She has incredible powers. One snap of her extra thumb and a whole army would appear. The three men outside would be the first to do her bidding.

She is the centre of the universe and all in it.

She is not mad Lear, hounded out by children, homeless, wandering from house to house, dogs at her heels.

Wherever she lives, she would be the Great Provider.

There is an extra joint on her right hand; she suffers from her joints. When she cannot walk, she crawls. What she cooks is got together from scratch by her. Even the sambar powder, used daily, starts with the pestle. She roasts her own coffee and grinds it out on an ancient manual grinder.

Each cup is fixed separately. This is a fine art, and so new to south India. Until recently, coffee was drunk only when ill. Yet they say, Nanjundan says, Thampi says, no one the world over can brew such coffee.

She has what no modern woman has, unquestionable proof of being the Great Provider.

Death or disease does not touch her. She is an idea. She is mother, father, everything. She is the object of all ancestor worship. She is the unfailing link.

To dissever oneself from her is to dissever oneself from oneself.

Nanjundan, poor Nanjundan, now I understand what it is to be Nanjundan.

He who has never known mammary glands can stand banishment better than he who has.

She is everything yet nothing.

She is the was of what shall be.

If you had her, I agree, nothing mattered, not plague, or parasite, not demon or danger, not ridicule or remedy, not anything not nothing.

Sreenivasan, Ramnath, Charu, Ranjan—they were all consistent in one thing. They could never resent their fathers. Is this true?

I covered my head with my *pallav* and touched her feet.

"South of Karnatak," she said, her face impassive, "only widows cover their heads." I could barely follow her Tamil.

Then unbidden, unseen by Nanjundan and all of hell, I knew how it was to be done.

Head uncovered I touched my forehead, my palms, my knees, my toes on the floor and paid my respects to her.

Brahmins living in cesspools, Brahmins with burnished metal for utensils, Brahmins whose houses stink of urine (because no low caste sweeper can enter their premises), Brahmins clinging fiercely to a genteel tradition, Brahmins keeping out the rest of the world (not knowing really that the rest of the world has an abundance of what they guard so fiercely); Brahmins, my friends, keeping aloof, fighting with poverty the attacks of modern progressives, living in a ghetto of refined filth, WITH ONE SUCH WOMAN, ONE SUCH AMMA, YOU HAVE WHAT NOTHING CAN DESTROY.

Born too late in time, I can never be her, nor she me.

10

WHEN I JOINED ANAND, I FOUND THAT WHEN CASTE Hindus invited me to their Hindu homes, if I touched a pitcher of milk, it usually went out of the window.

If a friend's mother visited me, she would bring her own glass, her own water, etc, and the only edible things I could ever offer them were fruit with the skin on.

At first, it was very hard to bear. The first time I noticed my touch pollutes anything on the dining table, I was dining with Ranjan's family—Kshatriyas—from the Punjab. The mother came from the third caste, and so I could not understand why. To test my observation I often reached out at the table and touched the roti, or beverage, or dal; each time it was taken away by the servants.

In Kerala, the Syrians believed they were Brahmins. The rajas of Kerala, as a recognition of their status, allowed Syrians on ceremonial occasions, a singular honour. Only the princes and royalty are allowed to eat on feast days on two banana leaves, one on top of the other, a mark of the aristocrat. A Syrian is allowed to bend the corner of his leaf as a symbolic double layer, approximating to the two leaves of the rajas! Whenever we fold one side of the leaf, we are aware of this fact.

Syrians kept aloof from every community, particularly Indian Catholics and Protestants.

To a north Indian, a Christian is a pariah converted in haste, usually from the scavenger class. The Christian ghettoes that are on the outskirts of every north Indian settlement are notorious for the "vices of the white man"; drink, women, and skin disease, a euphemism for a worse disorder. To a south Indian Brahmin (this I learnt only after I married Brahmin Nanjundan), a Shudra is preferable to a Muslim or Christian.

To the north Indian, the Muslim, though he is never to be trusted, has the magic of Urdu poetry and a courtly tradition, and the modes and manners of the two communities blend at the edges till it is hard to tell a Muslim voice from that of a Hindu.

As you travel south, beyond U.P., a Muslim is considered to be not worth an anna's thought. The only exception to this is Hyderabad where the last Nizam, often referred to as His Most Exhausted Highness (because he had as many wives as there are days in the year), gave the Muslim as much status as in the north. This was not merely because the Nizam was a Muslim ruler, but because the Nizam was the richest man in the world. If there is anything Hindu India respect, it is wealth.

The Brahmins were traditionally poor. So many of the professions were taboo for them. They could not really buy or sell, or go into any of the crafts. Learning Sanskrit or the Scriptures was not enough to make the Brahmins affluent, unless they owned temples. But Brahmin wealth is really of no use in practical living. Austerity is a ritual necessity. Even the use of wealth is ritual. It is limited to the number of diamonds women possess, the number of silverware in the household. Only silver is unpolluted. Crockery and cutlery made of any other material can only be used once, and has to be thrown away. Poorer Brahmins in south India discovered stainless steel, and christened it "ever-silver".

Since shoes are not allowed inside the house, carpeting too being impure, Brahmin homes look almost bare. The bed roll is rolled away, the bed frame stands bare. Anything exposed gets polluted. A Brahmin home looks as if the movers have come in. All rooms look like railway station waiting rooms. The living room is called the radio room, for that is all it sometimes contains.

South Indian historians love to write on Jainism in the south, Buddhism in the south, but there is a curtain on the Islamic contribution to the south. In this context, I understand the Syrian withdrawal from the cultural life of the south. It was not only a matter of choice but of necessity for survival. The Syrians became exclusive, amassed property, went into the professions; but they have no poets, no dance forms, no artists. Their ancient ways of leavening bread with yeast, using eggs for glazing, or spices for preserving fish or fowl indefinitely without spoilage—these culinary arts are their only mark of creativity. But it is typical that no one except the Syrian benefits from this.

The Hindus will not eat with anyone from a slightly different caste, and never under any circumstances from a Muslim or Christian.

Growing up as I did on an estate where every person who came there was either a serf or craftsman, there to serve you, I took it for granted that all the world knew that the Syrian was overseer, had money, land, physical energy, and was second to none.

I have also been raised on the impression that Brahmins were beggars. They were referred to as *pattars*, and *pattar*, I thought, was synonymous with beggar. Later, the Malhotras themselves aided and abetted in keeping this up; since they, influenced by the Muslim, did not care what the mother's caste was (unlike in the south where a Brahmin's offspring by a low caste woman becomes automatically a Shudra). The north Indian considers caste patrilineal, and this shook to the foundation the power of the Brahmin as an exclusive creature. A Brahmin is a ritual necessity in the traditional life of the north. But in recent years, a Brahmin has been just like a plumber or locksmith; he is sent for on occasions for a service, for ceremonies of death rites or marriages.

"Brahmins are most desirable," said Dr Malhotra, Ranjan's father, "as cooks, since food from a Brahmin cook is acceptable to all the castes." In this sense, a Brahmin mother is an advantage, if the father came from a lower caste. But the Malhotras, judging by their names, were on their father's side considered Kshatriyas, the second caste, but their mother was a Varma from the third caste. Yet, on ritual days they would send for the Brahmin peons of the Malhotra clinic, and distribute things like fruit and grain to them. *Pattar* equals Brahmin equals beggar; this was my understanding.

It came as a shock to me that Aiyar, who ran a fiction workshop, could with absolute conviction state that his antecedents took him five thousand years back, unsullied, untouched, unpolluted; that from the beginnings of history, he and his forebears had been the teachers, the priests, the learned. If the people of Jamrudpur were thieves by birth and breeding, Ravi Aiyer was a man of learning by birth—the highest caste, the least polluted, the purest, rarest, finest, all by birth, and thenceforth by breeding.

"How can you tell a Brahmin from a non-Brahmin?" I asked him. "Is there some physical distinguishable mark?"

Aiyar looks no different from a non-Aiyar. Someone, a critic, a friend of Nanjundan's, remarked that Shakespeare was talking about circumcised Jews when he said, "There is a divinity that shapes our ends, rough-hew them as we will," to mean that no matter how many foreskins are chopped off, nature will not take a hint.

Aiyar said, "a) the moment a Brahmin man, woman, or child opens his mouth, you know he is a Brahmin; his dialect is different, and no one can learn it at school, or ever approximate to it. No one, except a dumb man who is silent, can ever attempt to pass off as a Brahmin, but since a Brahmin's only function is verbal, no one can pass off as a Brahmin man.

"b) A Brahmin bathes differently, eats differently; he sits differently; his slightest gesture is distinct.

"c) Brahmin women are bred differently. A whole language of gesture, even the clarity of complexion, the quality of skin, is different.

"d) Brahmin food is chaste; you will get no odour of garlic or onion; no malodorous vegetables like cabbage will ever be cooked. Everything used in a Brahmin home is pure, as nothing is bought from outside, not even ground spices or prepared condiments.

"Pure, pure, pure, butter, its made at home. Coffee is ground at home and drunk traditionally only as a medicine. A Brahmin cannot touch alcohol, or smoke; he takes into his body nothing toxic. No human or animal decomposition pollutes him; traditionally, no skin, hide, or animal product entered the homes."

The nuances come to me now: If you see a man eating a watermelon, you may be sure he is not a Brahmin. They eat no fruit or vegetable coloured red; beets and tomatoes are out.

Why?

Blood, blood, blood, is red, not blue even for the bluest of blue Brahmin.

Language, that tool we use, is not merely magical as in the mantras; language shapes the mind as much as the mind informs the language.

It is not for nothing that Nanjundan is cerebral. The symbol takes the place of reality for Nanjundan.

I believe all this. It is in my nature to believe. Language shapes the human mind, not vice versa.

Would you believe it if I told you that a Brahmin has no vocabulary for genital organs, for human functions that are reproductory, alimentary or visceral?

That they have no language of sexual stimulation, and that they cannot express any emotion other than the ritual ones in any language?

A Brahmin copulates silently, or ritually, never realistically. Would you believe it—that Nanjundan who dreams in five incarnations, does not know the word for cunt, or cock, penis or vagina, except in embarrassed English, a language he learned from books?

When I got pregnant, I told Enid on the phone, "I am going to have a baby." I expected Nanjundan to be able to tell his friend Peter on the phone, "My wife is pregnant," but what did he say? He said, into the phone in my hearing, "I am going to have a baby!" It takes me years to explain this to myself, with the observation that he is a Brahmin and has no vocabulary for the middle muddle of human existence.

If there is no vocabulary for emotional input and output, if you cannot swear, or woo in a language, but if your words are set by tradition, and dignified by ritual contexts, then those emotions get sealed off and atrophy.

Word and flesh are like body and spirit; if you negate one, the other is crippled.

If a man were to blindfold himself for a few weeks, he would permanently impair his vision.

Nuances of experience are chipped, chiselled, cut round the edges, tailored to the Brahmin ideal by the Brahmin dialect.

Now don't ask me what came first, the word or the thing or the act it connotes as far as a Brahmin is concerned; let me tell you the words are given, and decide all.

All life is mantra.

All life is mantra, doing magic.

The word is never made flesh, but flesh must suit the word.

It is not that you suit the word to the thought but the thought to the word.

Maranam, sharanam.

Maranam, sharanam.

If I say that for a few days it will change me completely.

The power of the words is more potent than anything your Zen master can think up.

On the wedding night Nanjundan told me, "Your are ugly!" I became a beast.

A beast has several functions, but these functions, since they are alimentary and genital, are never acknowledged by a Brahmin, never mentioned, never dignified by verbal recognition.

If for ten days before the wedding Nanjundan made me cook round the clock, it continued for months after the ceremony.

He made me cook for Sunni; she is his life-long ideal. She works for him now. He said he cannot touch her because she is in love with another.

I hear from Kavita, that Sunni seduced a man in Delhi and told her fiancé of it. Sunni's fiancé is seduced by Kavita to whom he confesses that Sunni slept with the other man only because that other man reminded her of Nanjundan who has passion and imagination. Rung by rung, down the grapevine all desserts end up with Kavita. My mind boggles, there are labyrinths, morasses, I am being sucked under, I cannot keep my head clear of the maze. My dreams take on the contours of the day's doings. Every dream ends in pain. I wake in pain. I go to bed in pain. Meanwhile, femur to femur, the sexual revolution, but recently a fad in the west, becomes a way of life in Khilgesh.

11

THE STUBBY MIDDLE FINGER OF DR FRISK GOES UP MY rectum. He pushes and plunges. Everything moves up. I feel he is trying to deliver the baby through my throat. He seems to enjoy the rectal examination. Where are the Indians gone? Is this India?

"You are fully dilated," he says with extreme pleasure.

Each time his finger goes up, I scream. Sounds no longer come from my voice box, and pain, a scaffolding of wire-rope wound around each nerve fibre. Like gunpowder ignited at one end, it ran a million tracks of pain, faster than light. The message sent at one end was pain, the message received was pain; everything became pain.

Thirty-six times his finger goes up my rectum. I catch a thought that flashes through my mind. At Dachau where Dr Frisk was incarcerated by the Nazis, they had tied together the legs of women in labour....

Miss Stein, antecedents unknown, is fat and angry. She shaves my Mount of Venus. It looks now like the shaven head of a Hindu widow. She pushes a thick tube through my urethra. She curses, "My God! There is no opening, only a furrow," as she stabs at me viciously, I void in spurts on her hand. Miss Stein translates physiognomy into geography, and geography into racial estrangements. They take me to an x-ray room, leaving a trail of mucus and blood on tables and linen. Indian blood!

"A minor pelvis," mutters Dr Frisk. Get me an Indian doctor!

"Where's Papa?"

"In Bombay."

"I mean where's your husband?"

"I don't know."

He repeats the question. My answer is gargled out in screams.

They wind my feet in white linen; they tie them up to a stirrup.

I now become a public object.

Faces peer into me. I look between screams into the mirror below me.

My vagina opens like the mouth of a prehistoric mammal's, oozing blood, mucus, and placenta.

I long for a voice to call me by name, a hand to soothe my brow.

Masked red faces hover over me.

A super surgical light shines into my retina. My eyes know no rest. Each time they say, "Where's your husband?" I gargle out I don't know, I don't know, I don't know. They think it is a trap to get them, trap them. International experiments are all Nazi-inspired. Racial superiority.

Eight hours pass, they put something long and cold into me, I feel the sting of warm iodine rushing out. Breathe deeply, they say, and a mask drops me within seconds deep, deep, into darkness. I come to, fighting, screaming. Leave me alone, leave me alone, just leave me alone. I think of myself on all fours, crawling through a mossy undergrowth into a green, mushy pool in a forest. I am on all fours. They hold me down.

"You have a beautiful baby," sex unknown, does it matter? A child, a thing, a head, pain; "Take it away," I shout, my voice hoarse.

To feel that landslide of new emotions that now come up unbidden would be to finish the death I feel within me. Salmon give birth and swim five miles upstream and lie down and die. I am no longer I.

A nerve begins to twitch around my vagina. They make me get up. My head spins; my lungs stretch against my ribs. I creep to the toilet. I mess up my slippers. Faeces all over me. I creep to the shower and stand under it for hours, till they find me in a fever and in a dead faint.

As my fever rises, my hair stands on end, curled as if with a curling iron. The engorged breasts stand up like a surrealist object. The nipples are enlarged beyond recognition. The dark aureole is tipped with bloody marks, and gathers its intense stare of incomprehension. The veins around it look like so many rivers sketched on a map.

"You sometimes get fever when the milk flows," says Dr Frisk, trying to touch the breasts. I take his hand and try to throw it out of the window. Get me an Indian doctor!

I see the baby, a girl, with a deep gash on her button nose. She yawns in my face. My dead body revives. I am born again. She yawns again. As she nears my breasts, magnetic, she grabs with her mouth fiercely, like one fighting for breath. Pain bristles. They take away the baby still hungry.

"Such large breasts and so useless," says Miss Stein. I took at her flat breasts and feel no rancour. Go to Khajuraho, go to....

The nerve continues to twitch like a fish thrown out of a pond. Dr Frisk orders heat lamps strong enough to cook frozen hamburgers. I tingle with drops of sweat. I look at myself in a hand mirror. I see a red gashed valley and see in the glare of the heat lamp beads of sweat shine over the red exposed flesh.

Nanjundan turns up. He could not come earlier, he said, since he was helping Mrs Rajan write a review. Mrs Rajan, he said, is a middle-aged widow trying to make her way in life by reviewing.

"I admire her courage," he says.

On the tenth day, Nanjundan will not take us home; so I tell him on the phone that I am going to ask Aiyer, the professional Brahmin, to come and get us. Nanjundan arrives immediately. After he reaches us home, he disappears.

I am afraid the baby has stopped breathing. I can't sleep; so I drag the crib into my room. But the crib seems so far away. I put the baby in bed with me. I am afraid I would knock her over. So I sit on the floor with her. I am still sitting on the floor when Nanjundan gets home. He was helping Mrs Rajan with an article!

"I am sure you are making this up. There is no Mrs Rajan!"

"As soon as you are well, I am going to take you to meet her." But it takes longer than I thought to get well.

A waterfall of blood, a deluge of it, comes out of me. I am rushed to the hospital in an ambulance.

Nanjundan says with excitement, listening with pleasure to the siren, "Ah, this is the first time I have ridden on one of these!"

At the hospital, Dr Frisk is not there; his houseman is a Goan doctor. He caught hold of my uterus and pushed out several rubber sheets of blood.

He holds on to it; he talks to Dr Frisk on the phone, "No, no, no, it is not the stitches! I am holding on to the uterus!" He bangs the phone down. He says, "Holy Mary!"

I said, "Please don't let me die!"

He said, "Mother of God, we need angels here on earth!"

It is a beautiful moment for me. There is a haze, I cannot see too well, but my eyes focus on the doctor's face. I don't know his name. He sends for a sand-bag and straps it on my stomach. Later, they put three tubes into my arms and feed me drugs, and blood. I don't know the political antecedents of the donor; I am a trifle worried. They assure me, within weeks, there would be a conversion.

Nanjundan comes to see me; he stares at the woman in the next bed. He is overwhelmed. She reminds him of *Daphne with daffodils for hair.* I look at the woman. Yes, she is blonde. Most of Frisk's patients are Europeans.

Doctor Frisk operates on me. I don't see the Goan doctor again. They sterilise me, they stitch up all damages, they remove my appendix. Hours later, I come out of the emergency room. *Daphne with daffodils for hair* says, "Your husband's so cute. He was here with me till a few moments ago. He has gone out for a bite of breakfast."

"Oh? What did he say?"

"He said he'll be back."

When Nanjundan came in, I told him, "I think you should be with the baby."

"Mrs Rajan is with her. Nothing to worry about. I would rather be with you."

"I would rather you were with the baby."

"Suit yourself. Anything you say," and he walked out backwards. He did not take his eyes off *Daphne with daffodils for hair.*

Nanjundan never fails in minor things. He kept his word—he took me to dine with Mrs Rajan. She wears glasses, but is a good cook. They showed me to her bedroom where I am to sit with the baby. Conversation in the next room is low; I don't hear anything. At dinner the conversation is a bore. She gave me elaborate directions on how to make upma. I am bored to tears; on the way back in the taxi Nanjundan says to me, "I was thinking all evening how did I, by what stroke of luck, get hitched up with this goddess, my beauty!" I stifle my scream with the baby's cheek.

Kavita has published the story of her life—it ends with her married to someone like Nanjundan.

Kavita sees Nanjundan as a masterful man. One who knows his mind, one who never wavers. She turns to him in moments of confusion. He is her confidante. His chest is her comfort. In a world of uncertainties, Nanjundan is the one certainty. So, she married him in the book; though not in real life. Why?

In any case, what is all this to me? Have you a name for my condition? Dr Malhotra would have dismissed all this as nothing. Why am I not like Dr Malhotra? Is it because I am not a Hindu? Do Hindus have all the answers?

12

A BEARDED NEGRO WITH NATURAL HAIR, THAT CURLED UP like so many pincurls, stood leaning against the coffee bar. No stranger filled anyone with wonder at Khilgesh. But the sight of this American Negro did. He was bearded and dressed in an assortment of colours. A scarlet scarf was tied like a noose around his neck. His shirt was grey, over which he had a leather vest that bulged around the pockets. The Levi's was torn and tight, its colour splattered with mud. He belonged to the forest. He looked like a hunter. His nostrils flared.

Every now and again, he reached into his pockets and took out a banana and ate it. He had in his hand a sketchbook and charcoal. At first I thought the sketchbook was part of a public image. For did not art and the refinements come later in history?

His name was Rafael Ortez, he said. He stated it proudly. I tried to avoid his smouldering eyes. There was those rare occasions when it is difficult to look into a man's naked glance. The Lebanese girl, Miriam, all curves like the goddess Lakshmi, said: "He is harmless.

He stares at people." She seemed to be this wild bear's keeper.

The young man popped his eyeballs out and said, "That—is a stare."

"That's a glare," I said, trying to put my face on back.

She winked, so it looked like she had a nervous tic. She looked Anglo-Indian to me, and no authority on American Negroes or little Indian women.

I wanted to put her at ease; I shouted across, "You are from the bakery across the Mall!"

"Yes," she shouted, very eager. "I see you there."

"You are a child," said Rafael. I could not be an arrested case like Rahel. Innocence, like beauty, is in the eye that sees.

The Lebanese girl heard him. She said, "I always feel that Rafael's glance is like a laser beam." She was clearly afraid I would take this youth seriously. "Rafael, she has a child your age," she said.

Irritated, I said, "A person is as old as he acts."

Rafael laughed.

Now the Lebanese girl appealed to him, "She is old enough to be your mother."

Miriam is a glowing woman; she is a woman capable of feeling; he should be sketching her instead of me.

She said, "Whenever I fall in love, I prefer a man to be older. I don't care if he is twice my age, but if he is younger by even a year or two I feel like a mother."

I spoke to her now, "I am not looking for love, so I am free to talk to all ages."

The Ango-Indian women from the bakery stopped her tic.

I thought to myself, love? Have I ever known the meaning of that common word?

I used to say that when I touch black, I am back where I was born. But there are shades and shades of black, and shades of touch. According to Peter, there is a whole generation in America who unthinkingly mouth the words *Black is Beautiful*; he thought it was merely attitudinising.

As I talk to Peter, I get the impression that Negroes are the only real things in America. As real as the Mississippi, the river of initiation. I know I am a Negro at heart, would always be one. There was going to be no Africa of the soul to call my own.

The repetitive patterns in life are the first hint of the great cosmological joke we are a part of. One lost one's mythology the first time one learnt that hopping on and off a vehicle at the sound of a whip turns everything into a desert without an oasis. No memory is as strong as the memory of displacement, of dispossession. The heart is an empty machine. You can even transplant it. The muscle called the heart, that organ, that by tradition and experience changed the rhythm of its beats according to the tunes, the tones, the tensions, the syncopation of life's encounters, that was only a muscle, a machine. It was a thing. So were one's sexual machinery. If only one could detach one's *samanam* and parcel it by post to the right address. There would be time for refinements, like the touch of a hand on a tired brow, or the sound of a voice lulling you to sleep. Heart, heart, heart, went thump, thump, thump, but it could be donated, replanted, a tool common to man and animal.

Often I feel I am no longer in this world; I sit alone waiting for Nanjundan; no cars pass me; no light flickers outside; marriage has put a fence around me. Nanjundan said I am not to write any more. Nanjundan said I am no writer. Why does so much power reside in him? Does the fact that I open my thighs to him mean that no corner of me is exempt, no moment to call my own, no space that is my space?

Rafael's glance, glare, stare, marked the real-unreal lines between the haves and the have-nots. Speech, language, the gift that made man human, this gift marked the "scum" from the trash, said Nanjundan. The Brahmin from the Shudra, the poor trash from the rich trash. But a Negro was a Negro no matter what accents he spoke in, what dialect of the pure. The face of McKinley, the symbolic Negro visiting the mountain hideout of Khilgesh, comes back to me. His loud laugh, his wild laugh, had the tang of the ghetto, of hungers held in check. Speaking of an Indian writer, he said, "Did you notice his effeminate movements, half-man, half-woman? The shrill pitch of his voice, his long hair? He looks like a eunuch, his wife is from Kentucky, his first wife was a Swede. Dark races in search of blondes!"

If I have another beginning I will marry a Negro. I will get to the bottom of it. By marrying a Negro, you come into your inheritance. You also salvage what's left after the Empire, after the castration of your fathers, after every street in your land has been turned into public lavatories for the bootless begging cadavers who multiplied out of desperation, for the only joy left to a beggar is his phallus.

All over India they steal children; dozens of children are stolen each day, taken to other cities, starved, conditioned, and taught to beg, steal, and escape. Children as street arabs are a profitable business.

Only by living in the real ghetto of the soul, beyond tradition and expectation, beyond the century's jigsaw rat race, with every man's palm facing you, could you really be. To be a Negro is to be initiated beyond fear of loss.

"I admit," said the Lebanese girl, "That there are more important things than love."

"What for example?" said Rafael.

"Death," she said, "In Dostoevsky...."

"That's the trouble with you folks! You read too much...."

"Each man reads a different book," she said; she continues to talk about death, and how America had banished death from literature.

"There you go talking from books again! I have died a thousand deaths," he said.

"I have experienced death," she said. I looked at her face; it was flawless; her hazel eyes were ageless. "I have experienced death; do you know, it does not matter. I was quite ready to go. I thought of my parents," she said.

"Parents? What are they? That's something archaic!" I said.

"Though I have been raised in America I have been raised as if we were in the old country; my parents truly loved me. Not like my friend's parents; they merely gave their kids things."

Rafael started talking to me. He said, "Beauty is peace. Inner and outer. It is when everything is in its place. I see that beauty does not preoccupy you."

"Have you been at a wake?" said the Lebanese girl.

"Why are you obsessed with death?" Rafael snapped.

"I am obsessed with death," she said, like one really obsessed, "because we live as if we will never die."

He should be sketching her, I thought again.

"It is only the body that dies," he said quietly.

"Do you believe that sort of thing?" said Miriam, shocked.

"What sort of thing? It is light, that which you have. Light. Let there be light." He snapped his fingers. "It comes on and off like that!"

"I see that you smoke," he said to me sternly, with disappointment.

"I see that you pick your ears," I said.

"How long have you been sketching people in India?" Miriam asked.

"I sketch, I write, I am an expert on yoga, karate and judo. I also worked for the Living Theatre." His nostrils flared. "I am also interested in Indian music. Do you dance?"

"No," I said. "I hope you are drawing cubes and squares and circles."

"I am drawing what is inside you," he said.

"People draw the souls of cows before they can manage to draw the legs, four of them," I said.

"The Living Theatre!" said Miriam, and then she was in her element; drama was her specialty; it had brought her to India.

"I liked only one production of theirs. The way I see it is this. The nineteenth century asked an important question: Can the plastic arts express the aesthetic emotions of the mimetic arts? Can a statue scream? Now these people are asking the reverse—can the mimetic arts express the aesthetic emotions of the plastic? A necessary question, when you have plays that no one understands, but everyone enjoys. Now they...."

"I will tell you what it is," said Rafael, "it is body English. You speak with everything, words are only one small part of communication."

"Yes," said Miriam, in a trance, "the plague hits the cast; they die, shrieking, trembling, rolling like a slow glacier of death, real dying, gurgling like a sewer under a city, spilling like muddy water into a sea of faces no longer complacent. They are picked from all over the auditorium, stiff, stiffer than Egypt's mummies, placed five deep, forty bodies in a circle with a six foot diameter, then forty bodies become one body, and as the lights begin to change, dimming incandescent, they become like rock, sculpted with the stasis and rocklike immobility achieved by primitive art. If there was a God, he would find meaning in this; for we who have the same cells as all of life, return to make rocks, rolled forever round the sun."

The portrait was done; I glanced at it. The young man gave me a key to understanding my entire life. What an experience! My rudrakshi mala was there, and my bindi; what I saw hit me hard. "That is what I have met all my life!" Holy smile! Holy smirk!

I got up in a panic of understanding and said to him, "That is your ambivalence, not mine!" and fled.

Ambivalence, the word explained Nanjundan; it explained Mira, Rahel, everyone.

13

THE SUNLIGHT STREAMED IN THROUGH THE OPEN WINDOW. The afternoon like other afternoons sped on. I lay on my back, my mind lazily watching the shadow of leaves, when I began to feel being watched. I look sideways and see Nanjundan in the doorway of the bedroom to my right. He stood still, framed by the door. There was no sound or stir. He just stood there, not really watching me, and yet his eyes were fixed on me. He stepped forward, stiff-legged, walking strangely from the hip, his hands by his side. His eyes had a fixed immobility that began to reach me through my lazy, leaf-filled mind.

"Feel me! Feel me!" said Nanjundan. His hands were steel. His right elbow was on my chest, jabbing into my left breast.

His right wrist pressed against my collarbone, fingers wound around my neck. His left hand held my arms down. I thought lazily, why has he become a robot? Then I felt the pressure of steel. I was caught in such a relaxed position! I could not move; I tried to rise, but felt the weight of steel.

With each attempt to move, the weight increased, the steel tightened.

My mind was lazy no more, but frozen. I lay still. Very still. There was no specific expression on his face. His face was like his hands, like his legs, everything converged towards the pressure. I found it hard to breathe.

"I am not a thing," he said. It was said steadily. His voice too converged towards the pressure I felt. Though my legs were free; I did not feel the lower half of my body. Neither did I feel my head or face. I could not move any part of me. His voice continued on the same pitch, at the same pace, with the same weight.

"I am not an object. I am not a man without a centre. Feel me, feel me, I am a man of flesh and blood!"

"Nanjundan," I said, my voice now more girlish than I had heard it in ten years, "I want a cup of coffee. I want to drink a cup of coffee. Will you drink a cup of coffee with me?"

I kept repeating it. Calmly, quietly. I heard my own voice. It lingered in the sunlight and fell on my own ears with that unrecognisable quality.

As I lingered over the sound of my voice, his hands lost their stiffness. His fingers relaxed. I got up. My knees were like water. I knew then that my life had been in danger. I lay down again.

He patted me all over. Fingers straight out, he patted me with the palms of his hand. All over me. His hair flew in every direction. His face started twisting and turning, as though flesh and skin too could switch like hair. He said, "The fact is that you have married a very ugly man!"

Then his face contorted into an expression of rage; his pupils, round like agate marbles, spun so fast in a white disk that it seemed not to spin at all. He ran out, and into the kitchen.

When I could carry myself there, I saw his eyes shine with a brilliant light. It was the most extraordinary face I have ever seen. So full were his eyes that his pupils came upward, lightward, and bounced back thicker than light. An upsurge where heart-leaping-eyeward needed no object to behold but filled all objects. There were no lines on his face. Every cell filled out luminescent. And he said the following words:

"What you have seen is the death rattle of a husband. From now on I am going to be your friend!"

14

IN THE WOODS: UNDERFOOT THE GRASS IS DRY; LEAVES crunch and crackle. Bits of thorn and thistle stick to the edges of my sari. Occasionally I drag twigs with my *pallav*. I stub my toes. The land rises and dips, but the direction is clear. My back is towards the arches and cupolas and gargoyles of the Victorian Gothic behind me.

I stop to rest. I judge by the shadow of the trees that it is early afternoon. A nagging pain in my back makes me want to stretch out. I spread half my sari on the dry leaves and lie, down. Immediately, the trees seemed to grow in length; branches fill out; the sky itself is a vast expanse of other skies.

Nanjundan is turning out to be a fine nursemaid. He wants to excel me at it. But being my understudy, he cannot. He who was absent at the child's birth now plays mother. I cannot complain. Miriam considers me very lucky. She is raising hers, without the benefit of a man to help. She says—"If you tire of Nanjundan, let me know Mira." Nanjundan says that Miriam nursed me when I had the 'flu because she desires him. There has to be something I can believe in!

You out there, answer me!

—Gurus, Mahatmas, maha maha rishi. Dwelling on Kailasa or the abode of snow.

From Cape Comorin, Kanyakumari (another name for the nuns, my reverend sisters), to the mountains ridged out for view on relief maps of Bharat Mata, Rishi, Rishi, Guru, Guru, Hai Rama, Hai Guru.

Nanjundan paints female breasts, but he has put an eye on the breast, instead of nipples. Whose are those overseeing woman's breasts? Overseer, conscience, mentor, father confessor, guide, seismograph, this breast. Looking at a city, he says, "What would she feel about this city?" Looking at a man he says, "What would she say about this man?" Looking at a woman's breasts, he says, "What would she say, looking at my looking at these bobbing breasts?"

I want my breast back, and put my eye back in its sockets! He draws female legs, but he draws them white and hairless. They are always reaching out towards his Hindu hands, while he from one corner of his mind spins out those images that take the place of feeling.

He paints banana chips with bird beaks pecking. Banana chips, black dots whirling like dream fever, large human cells blown up by a clever photographer. Nanjundan, a middle middle child, wants to gobble up human cells.

Yes, I think carnivores emerge from Brahmin wombs, and they are suckled on milk, pure vegetable matter.

"A wheat cell," N. said, "is no different from a meat cell." All life is like the venus pitcher plant, unashamedly animal and plant, mineral and birdseed, and bird feather. What's faeces for one is food for another.

Now that he has tasted meat, he relishes human flesh.

Confessor! I confess. Murder will out. The river must reach the sea.

I see this landscape with the tree above me. An old man. Tall stoop and white beard. Skin soft to the touch like turtle eggs.

My mind whirls back to that priestly order of Jesuits, sparing brother Chacko the spanking he deserved because a carpenter's illegitimate son born out of wedlock died on a cross.

And what of Father Superior, father never mine, but of monastic house. Right Reverend. How right? How reverend? How father? How in God! Father DeCruz, bishop. Father Gomez, archbishop. Sometimes the lower classes usurp. The holy father, Pope Pius, was the most pious.

Priest! Venerable Bede long dead, along with Thomas à Kempis and Father Christmas.

O.M. is not Order of Merit but Old Man, Oldest Member, Doyen. Think, please, of hell as a sunset village with a jukebox and bowling alleys. Leading men, all elders to be sent there.

Father of the Church! Hear me and believe me. I am the word. I shall speak. You listen for once. Silence, as you say, is golden. In the Trappist regions of your soul behind the confessional mess, all you can say is, "I absolve you, go and sin no more." Too absolute is absolution, even from Fathers of the Church, whose loins rightly will never engender unless slyly, outside of the chronicles of such as me, as irrelevant as a Coca Cola sign in a novel of the interior.

Fatherhood is Christian; Fathers are always Christian Writers.

Fatherhood is this all-pervading all-powerful patriarch who is never available, always presiding, whose titles and powers and principalities run and outrun the space of all space, who always spilling over can subjugate. For those cheated out of this patriarchal deal there is always the Mahatma.

Mahatma Gandhi! The father of the nation is assassinated. I do not relish drink or food when his assassin is executed. See no Oedipus guilt in me, a woman. Did I not weep for that bronze figure of a criminal brought to that compound, dazzling white from the sand brought from the Kuttapuzha river? His cupped hands received water from a copper pitcher. He drank like a man who had crossed three deserts, and I wept as I watched that handcuffed, bronze-muscled, rippling golden horse of the sun, capable of dancing in paddy fields open to the sun, there glistening in the golden afternoon.

Listen to me, Father of English Poetry, Chaucer! Father of History, Herodotus! Father of Lies, dear endearing Lucifer! Tempt me not, temptations is doubt. Satan Lucifer says to me, "Nanjundan is crazy." And I say, "Nobody is crazy."

Early leader? How early? Does our leader's leadership and the mutiny and rebellion of our solar selves date back to that time when organ met organ and spilled and united? Out of three million possible me or you, the one possible, to emerge fighting. If one leads the other must follow, but aren't we all shaped out of the same clay, gendered by accident, nurtured by glands, spewed about by ancient regimes, mined from yellowing anecdotes of chronicled trees?

Progenitor! Does a transfusion of blood in a hospital change your political antecedents? Image of images, how many times removed from the original I ask you, sir biologist, Mr Nanjundan?

Fathers-in-law! The wise ones never miss contractual connections.

Stepfathers! Who come under the category of choice and adoption, I ask you: who adopts whom?

Originator! Please note that I am an animal with no beginning, no middle, no end.

Designer! Designing devil, architect of our intersecting venal blood, bluer than blue ink, and dwelling in ancestral embers, forever holding the posture of a particular moment for all eternity.

I am self-evolved—shaped out of nothing, gendered by accident; growing like manacles around me, an armour that laminates and holds a chink-proof convoluted evolutionist who knows that only the self is responsible for the self.

I have been talking aloud, addressing the hosts in the high dome. I have been speaking in tongues, frothing like a damned Pentecostal on quality words for fathership, fatherhood, fatherland, on city father, conscript father, and the rest.

But I hear now the crunch of footsteps, and I cannot make out why I am so worked up about a word that signifies less than nothing. The twigs crackle and I lie still. I raise my head, and in the distance I see a figure. Both real and unreal in its familiar gait. A man. A man with his chin buried deep in his chest approaches. Only his crown is visible. His pace is slow. His manner is like that of lepers and prostitutes when they are disapproved of by kith and kin.

His hair is spun flax. Light glints off it in every strand. He wears it long. What approaches me is flaxen hair, long, but polished with much brushing, like a woman's.

He is wearing tweed and an Irish linen shirt. I can see that. There is something about the figure that arrests, like a bone that turns up in a meat cutlet. He approaches. He does not see me. His feet are within a few yards of me. I lie still, mesmerised by the head of hair. He is about to step on me. He stops like a blind man who has been taught to feel unseen objects in space. He swivels on his heels to turn away and in that instant I shout out, "Peter Bradstreet!"

Like a man shot in the back, his head jerks up. His face is the colour of the undersides of turtles. The ridges run in circles, crustacean. The nose spirals sideways, one eye is lidded over and the other, larger than any human eye, gleams like the waves at Juhu on half-moon nights. Not pallor, not the flush of embarrassment, but the convulsions of delirium tremens chase in succession fear, panic, flight, pain, pride. He stops, silent. He seems to waver between raising his head and drooping his shoulders, and I hear myself say, "Peter, I have wanted to say this for some time, you can have me if you want me."

All ritual acts begin at the cerebral level.

He strips with speed. Drops his clothes under the tree. His body shines in the afternoon, unscarred as the day he was born. He seems more at ease naked. His *samanam* is long and sixty degrees up. My sari unlike Draupadi's comes off in a heap.

Immediately, his *samanam* is downcast, its one-eyed stare lidded. Lying on the ground I have a good view of it. A strange organ, its vertical gash like smiling lips, on a young old face.

"You must be patient," he says, in a voice that sounds like a tape played on the wrong speed. He spits into his hand, he fiddles, he fondles.

He gets dressed again.

I find myself speaking again. "For a long time now I have been thinking I must offer myself to anyone who will have me. Had I searched all over Khilgesh, Simla, or Delhi, I would not feel as I do now that touch is therapy. That your touch will restore me back to myself." My eyes are x-ray, my heart cobalt, and the interiors of all persons emerge and dazzle me. What I see is not Peter's face, but something that rises out and over, tall as this tree. So tall he touches this sky, leading to other skies—even that other sky I watched on the deck of a boat during the war when I saw Moses descending with his decalogue.

"I can now!" He spat into his hands. A man rubbing out the cold from freezing fingers, he lubricates himself.

He dives into me, he leaps up. Muscles tense and fill contours as with Puget and Michaelangelo. No Indian figure in granite temples moves with muscle. There, the dancing stillness of bodies are made to copulate with the help of fifteen maids holding the woman upside down, making god and granite and creature all one.

I feel now the vehemence of roots and tubers growing, and the persistence of moss rising around rubble, rising surely by sheer will. The tree spins like pipettes above me, drawing skyward the succulence of the earth. Something supernatural....

His *samanam* is no longer the tail of a nervous dog but a spear in the hands of one on a charger, golden in the sunlight of the body. The bronzed criminal brought to the white compound for a drink of water too had no fold or shadow.

Something marathon, I said to myself. For I am now silent. I am a spectator. I am also in the centre. All things are on the circumference.

He dives in, he leaps out. The pipettes about me spin blue and green and the golden horses of the sun gallop away and collect to brighten the western horizon.

There is suddenly a shriek, a groaning and frothing and shaking. I think of the epileptic outside my gate, *déjà vu*.

Tree and sky are now still. He moves as darkness descends.

"I did not know it was like that!" I said, my voice a whisper.

Leaning against the tree, pulling up his clothes, he starts roaring with laughter.

In the light of the dusk, his one eye gleams. He takes the end of my sari, a tie-and-dye one with spots of white on it, and throws it branchwards. "Sartorial disintegration!" he shouts. For a moment it flutters, festooning the air. The whites on the fabric show the light, still lingering.

He shrieks with laughter. Everything echoes his burst of cracked sound. There is a final echo, lower—but harder to describe. It is Nanjundan's. He has arrived, looking for me.

We start speaking in unison. We speak in different voices, at different speeds. I am trying to get dressed. Nanjundan is busy trying to invent in Malayalam, "One, two, buckle my shoe." Peter rehearses a curtain speech. I am muttering the mantra I had made up earlier. *Maranam sharanam*, death surrender, death surrender.

Onnai, randai
one, two,
entha pennai
what girl!
munnai, naalai,
three, four
chirukunnuenna!
why laugh!
anchai, aarai
five, six
entha saarai!
what sir!
ezhai, ettai
seven, eight
kaito chaita!
listen brother!
onpathu, pathai
nine, ten
ayo pothai!
o my buffalo!
pathinonnu
panthrandu
eleven
twelve
anda gundoo...
kakoooo
Kandau!
anda gundoo...

m
a
r
s a
a n
r a
a m
n
a
m

a a a
m r n m
m r n m
a a a

m s
a a
r r
a a
n n
a a
m m

r a n
a a
s m
m m
a a
r a n

a a a
s r n m
s r n m
a a a

s
a
r
a
n
a
m
a
n
a
r
a
m

If I knew
all
life
would be
wiped out,
viewed
by
absolutely
no
one,
I'd
see
to
it
that
my
last
and
therefore eternal
posture
would
be
admirable:
think
of
that!
meditate
on
it! ...

Nanjundan comes home early in the morning. His back erect, his shoulders square, his skin stretched tight; his smile is clearly not a grimace.

He comes towards me and says: "Peter says you have no shame."

"No shame; maybe I should go out and buy me some!" I said.

"Mira, you must not think I am trying to usurp Peter!"

"Nanjundan, how can you usurp Peter, you are not a woman!" and he says "Oouuuuu-Nooouuuuuuuuu!" and rushes out of the house.

I begin to pack in haste; I must take that road from nowhere to nowhere, and keep my date with what's to come.

15

THE LIGHTS OF SAN FRANCISCO BAY SHINE ACROSS A smoking chimney.

The city hums with the sound of life.

A butterfly flutters into the room. There is immediately a stillness in the room.

I think of the butterfly on the town bell in a haiku.

The smell of tobacco lingers in the room like memory. Outside the house, the streets run vertical instead of horizontal, just as in Khilgesh.

Leaves swirl up and down the hill. At the foot of the hill is the world's tallest eucalyptus grove.

A face with high checkbones reflected in the window is familiar, unfamiliar.

Everything is beautiful, the baby too. We have been travelling, to the antipodes, across meadowland and oceans belonging to continents, across snow-capped mountains carved into temples of stone.

In Bharat, India, millions of cows straying away from meadowland eat billboard signs on thoroughfares and survive with bovine grace.

Miles of meadowland tilled by men turn machines into men.

Children of all ages love beautiful things.

Once I saw a Shudra woman with beautiful feet shovelling moth wings. The Shudra woman with beautiful feet shovelling moth wings saw one moth asleep over the mantelpiece.

Survival is not only possible, life is possible in the here and the now.

A girl hardly in her teens, walking along Telegraph Avenue on the arms of a young boy who has not yet begun to shave, smiles at Baby; America loves an infant and smiles.

The young girl has on her forehead a sticker from an old book, red on yellow; the single word on the sticker reads, USED. I laugh. I am pretty sure we are all the same.

An old woman, her face a parchment, comes towards me; tall Americans stride past me, but she comes up to me; we are eye to eye, and she says, "Oh, you marvellous people we are so big and you are so little!" I laugh.

We are all the same. I tell myself. Everyone has the same joys and anxieties. The moment after and the moment before. Pre and post. Memory, that wonderful granary of the mind, that is what is divinely human. Gather ye while ye may. Does it matter that two hundred and ninety-seven people leapt off the Golden Gate Bridge? I know I never can. Though the thought of this stung my nerves like the lit end of a cigarette, visions of the velocity of water and wind below, head on collision, and instant release turned somersaults in my mind, beyond the bridge there danced on the waves, a paradise called Alcatraz—once filled with the breath of criminals, now standing empty, a garden fluttering with colours—and the sea with its benediction of spray, blues flecked with white, floating real-unreal on walls of waves.

Being put away on such an island is not being put away at all. It is like getting lost in a garden of your favourite fruit—say persimmons.

Alcatraz is empty.

Once, to think was to feel and to feel was to know.

Now to know is the loss of feeling which gives rise to thought.

Even as I shape this desperate thought, a passing Negro with dancing eyes and a straw hat says to me, "I believe, I hear, that this country once belonged to you Indians. Now they have taken over Alcatraz!"

"Who has?"

"The Indians have; which tribe do you belong to? They would be happy to welcome you. In fact you can easily join them."

I laugh my loud laugh into the sky; I can sail to Alcatraz and join my tribe; I have always thought, "Give me an island and I can be Pitt the Younger." I thought that till I too was twenty-four. Now ten years later, I no longer want to be queen, but I know how to walk like a queen.

I reword my own words: "To be born is to feel, and to feel is to know. To die is to lose feeling which banishes thought."